THE REPROBATE

A novel by
David Dow Millar

A telling tale about how the right instincts and traits can allow someone to succeed no matter the circumstances or the absurdity of the risk taking to achieve desired goals.

Individuals with a complete disregard for everything deemed civilised can thrive and do accomplish their dreams with the connivance or the mutual benefit of others. They seek out fragile people by instinct and are indifferent to the chaos they leave in their wake.

The veneer of civilisation cloaks their activities. They travel through all milieus in their search for someone or something to exploit. Observing the banality and self-delusion that lies behind all social structures, they manipulate anyone seeking reassurance. To expose them means admitting that the moral basis of modern living is a complete utter lie.

This is a story about such a reprobate and his women.

First published in Great Britain in 2015
Copyright @ David Dow Millar 2015
First Published 2015 by The Misty Tree
The moral right of the author has been asserted
All rights reserved.

ISBN 978-0-9929340-4-0
EBook ISBN 978-0-9929340-5-7

DISCLAIMER

All characters and places mentioned in this novel are fictitious and any inference to real people, dead or alive, is coincidental. Any familiarity is simply because most people's lives and events are similar, and the interpretation is only different.

This is a tale about extremes and depravity, about the silliness that some people get away with and the pain others bring upon themselves.

A reminder that amoral people unless forcibly stopped have no limits and will take advantage of anything for their own ends. Maybe, just maybe, their strong self-interest mechanism stands them out as superior beings destined to win the evolutionary race that dictates the progress of man. Moral indignation of their behaviour may just be after all jealousy while wearing a halo.

In the meantime, if you are a comfortably well-off parent with an unloved, vulnerable daughter, a chancer may soon be paying a visit to prey on her frailties.

CHAPTERS

"The pious pretense that evil does not exist only makes it vague, enormous and menacing. The confessions of Aleister Crowley, Occultist"

THE REPROBATE

Alfredo Mascagni, a pale-skinned Italian, only left his lodgings ten minutes earlier but already had reached the outskirts of the mid-twentieth century built commercial part of town. The streets become broader and busier here as he approaches the main confluent of road arteries that come together at a large island roundabout full of rhododendrons and other large display plants. A haven for bird and insect life as no fox or cat could ever navigate across the perpetually busy traffic lanes. The din and smell of the traffic act as a barrier to nature's own opus. No scent distinguished from the trapped flora, nor bird song heard, sometimes there is the faint hint of iodine hitting the nasals before any sight of the English Channel can flood the eyes. Alfredo's objective that winter's morning was on the other side of the isolated natural oasis via a long echoing pedestrian underpass.

Alfredo has a bulldog physique: a strong-boned powerful man of average height with only a trace of a neck, a man of forty or so. Middle age has given him a rounder figure but it has not diminished the fierce fire burning in his green eyes. Today he deliberately made himself appear dishevelled and down on his luck by not washing or shaving and by wearing put aside worn out clothing for such an occasion as of today. Gormless thick-rimmed round clear glass spectacles framed his round bald head covered by a small army green woollen cap. His exaggerated stride reminds you of a great ape. The sighting of the underpass appears to signal the slowing down of pace and the start of a limped walk that to a good observer seemed to displace itself from one leg to the other. He wore faded brown cord jeans and a light blue denim top under a heavy tweed jacket that zipped up at the front. On his feet, a fashionable pair of dark blue denim baseball boots with red stars on the sides.

The Italian resides in a peaceful and well-off south coastal town known for its agreeable climate and excellent social life. Hayes-by-the-Sea is a place, which has not seen snow for at least forty years, where the young and successful liberals flock to build safe havens for themselves and their declared alternative way of life. For the other townsfolk, it is a jolly good place to live where the life expectancy is well above the national average. Bad or unsettling things rarely happened. No one died from poverty and it was not considered a romantic spot for suicide. There are the usual problems of the old slowly dying alone, isolated in their homes and the young overindulging in drink or driving their cars too recklessly along country roads but it was no worse or better than elsewhere. No ambitious police inspector would apply to serve here.

Sheltered on each side by chalk cliffs the town resting on a gradual sloping plain had its own microclimate.

The wearing of knitted beany hats, scarves and gloves in winter are more of a fashion statement than the real need to keep out health threatening cold. The skies are rarely dark and broody for long, no persistent terrible frosts to chill the bones or slipping on treacherous black ice cracking limbs to cause untreatable niggling pains there forth. Squirrels are not obliged to hibernate. On the other hand, the children of the town never knew the joy of snow, no snowball fights, no slides, no snowmen to guard the house at night; nor opportunity to reap innocent revenge on miserable killjoys, who stopped ball games near their precious cars, by squirting water into keyholes, which soon froze car door lock mechanisms.

The town was once just a fishing village that was infamous for enticing vessels to sail onto nearby sandbanks. The most notorious of such occasions occurred in Elizabethan times when the entire crew, man and boy, of a stranded Portuguese galleon were butchered. A time when the civilized world declared that this country was a pariah state led by apostate rulers. The town would expand into a fashionable seaside resort in the late eighteenth century due to its health given air from mineral-laden wind blowing in from the sea. It expanded again after the Second World War to accommodate the demand for cheap working-class holidays. Then like most seaside resorts, it went into decline. However, the bed and breakfast hostelries did not succumb to enticing the socially unwanted from other towns to come and claim benefits. No dead-end streets, no one born here could allege they came from a financially deprived background. The town itself never suffered the blights resulting from years of industrial pollution from heavy engineering or factories bellowing out caustic black smoke. Over the last twenty years prosperity has returned and the old part of town has been transformed into an artisan paradise which attracts the day tourist again and students from nearby universities to enjoy the galleries, the second-hand bookshops, antique and food fairs, good organic restaurants, gastro bars and all the other paraphernalia associated with comfortable living. The modern pretty young things residing here now would be instantly recognisably by a reincarnated Evelyn Waugh.

The names of the streets and lanes in the old town reflect its origins perfectly. There is King George's street leading into Corn Market square where the historic structure is now an Art Centre with a small theatre for showing continental films and touring plays. Nearby, Queen Anne's street runs into Regent's street near the memorial to Lord Nelson, while Old Church road takes you towards the harbour and the Custom House, now converted into a local tourist office. The unpretentious structure of the church that once stood out on an isolated promontory to allow it to be seen from the land and sea is now lost within the expanse of the town. Its graveyard populated with weather worn tombstones that barely proclaim the names of displaced Huguenots and families of the new commercial class that saw their younger offspring fought at Waterloo or sailed the seas searching for evasive French and Spanish men-of-war, or worse still spending years with the South Atlantic squadron in desolate cold waters. The impressment of ordinary locals as navy ratings is remembered by the aptly named Press Gang 's snug along the old quay, near the old fisherman mission and the defunct lifeboat slipway.

The roads out of the old town indicate once there were ancient woods and then parklands, names such as Woodlands road and Elm Street. The different architectural periods give the place an eclectic organic feel. The once neglected elegant Georgian Palladian and classical architectural houses are now comprehensively renovated and sparklingly clean. The era of the buildings is instantly recognisable because of their well-known symmetrical appearance with their elegantly dressed doors and windows. These early and late Georgian buildings coexist in tight narrow streets or surround picturesque garden squares. Squares that have had their rigid structures restored to reveal manicured symmetrical gravel or stone paths through slightly raised flowerbeds and lawns to a central decorative feature like a fountain. All this exists within a distinct historic district next to the time-proven storm proof old stone harbour with its derelict period fish auction and salting sheds, and other disused warehouses. These older buildings have brick frontages intermingled with exposed wooden beams. Some of them have large decaying double-sided oak doors swung open to reveal rotten wooden vaulting over weed infested alleyways that lead to unloved enclosed inner courtyards. This dereliction contrasts vividly with the restored Georgian part of town, where it is rumoured that Jane Austen spent a few days dwelling at the George and the Dragon inn. In the early twentieth century, a tired Arthur Conan

Doyle visited the town on a tour of the coast looking for a spot to finally end the career of his literary nemesis.

The outer districts have remained relatively the same in recent times continuing to be quiet dormitories for raising families to supply staff for the commercial service industries and the many old folk homes scattered around town. They are mostly the standard two up and two down dwellings with small front and back gardens. Each district has a small shopping precinct with the usual assortment of shops at key points. These are places where relatively young couples prematurely age themselves by conforming to the role of homeowners with smart well-cut lawns, believing an expensive car and luxury kitchen are *raison d'etre* for living. The architecture in the designated top end executive quarters is the standard detached house with its own little green belt protected by mature thicket or high brick walls.

The town is also a dormitory for a large casual workforce required for the surrounding agricultural enterprises: a healthy contingent of young eastern European workers who commute out of the town every day to help grow and pick crops in nearby large commercial farms. At night, they hang about near the old harbour area to pass the time in the open rather than being stuck in their clamp abodes. They mainly stand around chatting or drinking cans of lager imported from their home country, sold by a nearby corner shop that only survives by catering for all their needs.

The seafront has never been a major selling point for the town. Better beaches along the coast attract people. Although in recent times, the rise in interest in natural sciences has seen it get more attention. However, the exposed hard on the feet pebbled beach generally fails to entice bathers and it remains the principle domain for wildlife, keen amateur fossil hunters and brave dog walkers, especially so in sporadic severer winters when a bracing breeze can come off the Channel. The only time it tends to attract greater public interest is when sea creatures like pilot whales, dolphins and leatherback turtles get stranded due to getting trapped in discarded nets or being confused by shipping traffic noise, then the ghoul watchers come out in force.

It is an early Tuesday start for Alfredo. The letter received last week from the local social security office invited him to attend a review of his circumstances at eleven in the morning. No other details were supplied except a demand to bring as much identification as possible with him. He is unperturbed by this request as he had attended many of such reviews in the last five years or so. At the office, he is told to go to his normal spot and sit down until he is called. He takes his place next to the usual assortment of claimants and ponders about nothing in particular. There are young mothers with their charges playing on the floor. Some migrants waiting patiently for a freelance translator to arrive to explain how the process works. Casual workers periodically requesting aid and the experienced know everything there is to know about benefits that can be claimed. Alfredo is one of the latter and is acquainted with most of the staff by their first name.

It is a typical social security office. The main entrance leads straight to a reception desk positioned straight in front of a large open plan area. A reception desk sporadically staffed to direct any waiting claimant to the scores of zones with their own set of duplicated desks and seating. A security guard stands permanently near the entrance and tells any querying claimant to wait at the reception desk until addressed by a member of staff. At each of the different seating zones, a well-displayed sign explains the consequences of rude or violent behaviour aimed towards any of the staff. There is also a touch screen terminal available to conduct basic job searches while you continue to wait. Upstairs there is a maze of corridors leading to private offices for the staff and formal interview rooms.

When Alfredo sees Janice and Betty coming out of a staff only door that takes you upstairs he assumes that he will soon be interviewed. The staff sit down at their desks unhurriedly organising themselves. Alfredo smiles at them as they take their seats, behind desks stacked with folders and a large PC. Betty completely ignores the gesture of friendship as she considers him to be smarmy and a parasite. It is obvious that it is an intended policy to delay service to ensure that the claimant spends adequate time on the premises. Primarily to make them appreciative of any claim granted to them and just as importantly also to disrupt any undeclared black-market activity that some may be engaged in. These two women have been working as a team for many years now. Their good cop and bad cop routine was well known to Alfredo who takes delight in second-guessing what will be said next. They are casually dressed in clothes suitable for middle-aged women: cardigans, thick patterned cotton blouses and hardwearing slacks. He always imagines that they are much older than him but in reality, are of similar age. Janice is the good cop and comes across better educated and social worker-like whereas Betty is obviously a straight from school take no nonsense person. One gives the claimant the benefit of the doubt for a missed signing on time or when there is no clear evidence that showed any recent attempt for finding work. The other just assumes the worse and that the claimant is untrustworthy and not serious about finding work. Her experience has taught her that the thick never realised that their schemes to defraud others for cash were obvious.

After a few minutes, Alfredo unexpectedly hears his name called from another direction. A smartly dressed young woman stands waiting for him near a staircase at the far corner of the floor. He wanders over to it and follows this woman upstairs, contently focusing on her backside as it swings side to side in a tight black skirt. A couple of sharp right and left turns causes disorientation and eventually places him in front of a strong pine coloured fire door with a small plaque informing him that it is private interview room, number five. The young woman simply knocks on the door then swiftly walks away.

After a delay, a male voice beckons Alfredo to enter. The room is carpeted with a delicately speckled design on a navy-blue background. It contains the customary teak desk and several uncomfortable hardback laminated chairs. A couple of bland photographs decorate the dark grey walls. The two occupiers are smartly dressed in top of the range formal suits. Although initially taken back Alfredo quickly resumes his indifferent air and sits down without being asked. The purpose of the interview is explained in a matter of fact manner. Some anomalies have been found and they would like more background detail on his upbringing to confirm he is who he purports to be. Their accents suggest they are more likely to be from up town rather than from the local area.

Alfredo explains that he had come over as a child to this country with his parents when they left northern Italy near the Swiss border in the province of Varese to take up a new life working in a ceramics factory that produced wares for the restaurant industry. They were hard working skilled workers who hoped to give their only son a better life. Unfortunately, they passed away without being able to leave him with a financially secure future. He passes over all his documentation while continuing to recount his family's background. He went to a local school in Railhead, when old enough headed up town to earn his way in life then left the great hub to seek a life abroad before eventually returning to the south coast. His adventures became that of an itinerant worker as, in his own words, he was prepared to do anything for food and shelter. He put his hand to bricklaying, painting and decorating, crop picking and renovating farmhouse properties.

It is pointed out to him that his official work history

states he had only managed to achieve one month worth of national insurance contribution in his whole life and that although at first sight his identification documents looked valid they are actually just good forgeries. Unperturbed, Alfredo explains that he has been unlucky with bad health and had hoped the better air here would aid recovery or at least alleviate his health problems. In his last working adventure, abroad he fell off a ladder and landed on stony rumble. This accident damaged the ligaments in his left leg, upper arms and did his back in. It has severely handicapped his ability to do manual work ever since. As far as any possible forgeries are concerned he does not know what they mean as he just remembers finding his Italian birth certificate in a drawer in the house of his now departed parents and had always innocently assumed he was allowed to claim benefits as a naturalized subject. His parents not fully understanding how the system worked maybe unknowingly caused the unfortunate misdemeanours. They did come from a chaotic Italian background so they probably wrongly assumed that bureaucracy here was relaxed as well. Alfredo smiles while giving these possible explanations for the anomalies.

The officials ask him if he has any photographic proof to demonstrate his wherewithal. Alfredo flips open and quickly closes his wallet to give a glimpse of a travel card. A hand grabs his wrist to prevent the wallet from being drawn away to allow closer inspection. It is pointed out with asperity that the travel pass is just a complete amateurish counterfeit as all he had done was paste his own photo over that of the genuine recipient for this purloined civic subsidy for seniors. He is also obviously too young looking as well. It is all just a blatant and unsubtle disregard for the social system and public purse of this country. Only an idiot or maybe an inscrutable chancer would have the nerve to conduct such frauds. Alfredo remains unabashed by these accusations being emphatically aired at him.

An incredulous civil servant then smiles tilting his body backwards against the chair. His partner takes a packet of cigarettes out of his pocket, ignores the non-smoking legislation, lights three cigarettes, and offers everyone one. It is a brand that Alfredo enjoys and the friendly offer is not refused. All this signals that the preliminaries are over and it is time for business. The truth is that they are not interested in any social security swindle or any other nefarious dealings. They know his real identity is Steve Crow the local councillor for the Morley ward here in town. Visibly affronted by this outrageous accusation, Alfredo laughs at the absurdity of it. He restates dates and facts about his past and volunteers names of local people to confirm his identity. The relaxed smiling expressions on the faces of the accusers indicate that the bluff has made no impact. All pretence is finally dropped when presented photographs show Alfredo transforming into councillor Crow.

The interrogators explain that all his entrepreneurial activities shall be overlooked and kept out of the public domain so long as he agreed to be helpful. Their bosses understood only too well that no one was perfect. As far as they are concerned he can continue life as usual and only has to send routine surveillance reports to them. In fact, a basic retainer payment of four hundred pounds a month with appropriate bonuses for any good information received about political colleagues or even rivals will augment the currently received benefits for the bogus Mr. Mascagni. If he refuses to help then this interview has never happened and criminal court proceedings will immediately commence to obtain justice, recoup illegal earnings and end all political ambitions.

Steve easily accepts their kind offer, as he is very happy to be of service to the nation he loves. It is his duty to help safeguard the populace from extremism. Produced official secret act declaration papers are then signed on all the indicated dotted lines. The recruited informer will be the eyes and ears on the ground in Hayes-by-the-Sea to report anything suspicious. To show eagerness and the right attitude, Steve asks if he has a designated codename and what department does he come under. Is it MI5? Taking no notice of these flippant questions, it is explained that his bogus name will be his ID and its acquired national insurance number shall be requested to confirm his identification. Instructions are given on what to look out for, how to report and send information via an easy to remember social security address; there is also a use once only emergency phone contact while regular face-to-face meetings will always occur in this office building. All his false identification documents are given back to him when the meeting ends with strong friendly handshakes.

Outside, Steve quickly realises the benefits of this

unexpected new role. A role obtained by chance due to his bold foolhardiness in his manner of obtaining something for nothing. Any possible disadvantages are not considered; only potential gains are brought to mind. The basic financial gains will not make much difference. He would have to think up some good tales to gain the extra bonus money. However, he will be allowed to continue claiming well over one thousand a month on rent and disability benefits. The protection of the state means no more fear of prosecution, no need to hide or spent arduous effort camouflaging his activities. In addition, there is the potential of removing foes by supplying malicious gossip about them to his minders. So long as they get consistent information that conforms to their views of others, then his position should be safe and he will be a valued protected property of the state. He stretches his limbs, tales off the glasses, immediately grows in height and radiates a self-confident disposition. His stride is more dominated by a raised chest than primeval arms swinging. The idea of a full English breakfast with a pint of beer to nicely round off the morning enters his head. He never eats a fry-up at home purely because it is cheaper and easier just to eat out rather than go to the effort of buying ingredients and cooking them.

This contented man has many good pubs to choose from as he saunters back east towards the old part of town. The destination is a frequently visited hostel, down a cobbled one-lane side street, called the Volunteer. Its hanging pub sign shows the front profile of a Georgian gentleman with a felt hat on his head, a long musket in one hand and a satchel of powder and ball over the opposite shoulder. The pub is a revamped traditional dark oak wooden structure with a corner bar that has high shelving displaying rolls of clean glasses. An open staircase leads to a gallery while the toilets are located at the back past the door leading to an enclosed yard that catches the sun in the mid-afternoon. On the walls are posters of previous and future folk and indie rock events in the area. On the morning shift is Carol, an attractive long sandy-haired thirty-something divorcée. She is wearing her regular tight blue jeans, white blouse and a small black apron around her waist. The outline of her bra containing an ample bosom is as usual conspicuous.

Steve orders the large all-day full English breakfast with a side portion of chips, extra toast along with a pint of a locally produced special bitter. As he waits for the food, he chats idly with Carol and the other bar customers about known regulars and their current activities. At one of the tables, a young pale looking woman sporting bright purple hair and a diamond nose ring is heard saying thank you for a good time to a tall skinny coke drinking light-skinned African as she bounces out of the pub. One of the customers, a young artisan looking fellow, suggests there must have been a party last night. The barmaid chips in by saying that there is a party here every night. When the steaming hot breakfast of double portions arrives, the others look on with envy as the hungry Steve sits down and devours it. Carol says she would not like the job of feeding him as the last morsels of bread wipe the plate clean. The demolition is exaggerated by smacking both hands on his extended stomach

followed by the downing of the remainder of his pint.
He must now weigh double what he did before.
Returning to the bar, a fifty-pound note withdrawn
from a back pocket and placed on the counter
indicates his willingness to pay the food bill and have
another refresher.

A couple of hours later he arrives back at the flat,
which is situated just north of the old town and in
easy reach of all its facilities. It is a first floor three
bedroom flat with high ceilings and box-shaped rooms
within a refurbished townhouse. The original grand
Georgian entrance hall is communal space and the
best feature of the building. He enters the flat quietly
as possible as it is too early to disturb Mi-Cha as she
will be at her peak of productivity in the backroom
that has been meticulously converted into her place of
work. The hallway walls are decorated with an
eclectic mix of oriental artefacts and drawings along
with framed photographs of Iron Age sites. A finely
braided bamboo sheath intended for a replica
ceremonial sword hangs near the well-built secure
main door. In case of emergencies, it houses an ever-
sharp machete.

Steve will chat to Mi-Cha when she rests prior to
recommencing her work later that evening. She is a
Korean in her late twenties who has known Steve for
over five years since they met up at Art College. She
had specialized in arts and crafts, creating ceramics
and beaded jewellery. Reproductions of old
earthenware designs and household jugs rather than
attempting to create the highly polished finish found
in the established factories. Her Oriental and Celtic

beaded jewellery skills gave her knowledge of knot making that any old sailor would have been proud to possess. Where there is the artist you will find inherited wealth. In this case, her father is an executive back in Korea with a well-known electronic company who continues to help fund her and Steve's spending. If the rich have too much money he will happily find ways of spending it for them. Her father financed the buying of the flat and a buy to let property further out where his doppelganger officially resides with the other single roomed tenants. In Steve's worldview, people who just work all their lives and hoard their wealth deserve to have it taken away from them.

Most of Mi-Cha's income from her own activities is gained through agency work so she has to comply with the bureaucratic state regulations and rules on how work can be conducted and accept that the agencies take a fair chunk out of her earnings. Nevertheless, she is the biggest wage earner bringing in over a thousand a week. Steve's activities return about six hundred and rental income is in the order of four hundred a week. They are not real millionaires yet, only paper millionaires, but under the guidance of Mi-Cha it is a team effort to get there. Steve likes the fact that Mi-Cha has the American idea of western values and not the wishy-washy hypocritical British ones. Having a strong disposition to veracity no matter if it is unpleasant or disagreeable, Mi-Cha is incapable of deluding herself. She rarely argues or takes a bad mood out on anyone, and has quickly accepted that no children will come out of her relationship with Steve. With regards to attaining wealth, it does not matter to her how it is acquired only that they had it. If you did not have money you were nothing.

The couple normally spent most of their downtime in the kitchen, as it is always warm and intimate there due to the Aga and the many well-used utensils that Mi-Cha loves. She is a westernized oriental that assumes the role of cook and homemaker. The correct shade of sky blue adorns every built-in and stand-alone appliance. Even the ash wood cupboards inlaid with shaded glass panels have matching coloured sky-blue glass and sky blue ceramic handles. Thick rustic terracotta tiles cover the whole floor. A gantry hung from the ceiling extends the full length of the kitchen packed with all sorts of pans. The large American style fridge is plastered with postcards and family pictures of Korean relatives dispersed all around the world. A family evangelized during the height of the north-south conflict to have a strong right-wing American Christian faith. Oriental genes combined with Protestant work ethics to produce a tremendous hard-working ethos within all members of her family. The most obvious effect of a strict conservative patriarchal upbringing on Mi-Cha is a natural obedience to male authority. This made her vulnerable and the perfect type of woman that Steve could subjugate.

Steve makes himself a cup of filtered coffee, sits at a wide solid light oak kitchen table facing the closed door and gets his smartphone out to make some business and social calls. He first phones his full-time assistant at the council. The assistant handles all the paperwork and he only phones to ensure that nothing extraordinary requires his attention. After asking her if she was fine and how things were going, he gets her to confirm that today's paper and electronic mail had been worked through and any grievances have been passed on to the correct departments. They then discuss how much of last week's expenses can be put through the charity trust account intentionally setup when he became a councillor to minimize tax payments and how much had to just be fully paid out of his allowances. He coaxes the assistant to by-pass financial protocols to include some dubious expenditure under charitable expenses. The next phone call is to Julia telling her he will be around her place that night at the usual time.

Presently, a tried Mi-Cha enters the kitchen to prepare dinner, chicken and noodles with a raspberry cheesecake for dessert. She is naturally prone to fatigue due to her small light frame. Her head is almost perfectly round like a cute china doll with large shining black eyes that dominate her face; currently exaggerated even further by her short boyish hair. Her small breasts and tight backside combined with her bold hairstyle suggest a person much younger than her actual years. It gives her an alluring nymphet look. Steve gives her a wet kiss intentionally leaving his tongue in her as she draws away. Talk turns to work and he asks if she is dealing with her regulars or are any potential new customers showing an interest. She replies that it is mainly regulars and did not think further expansion is practical unless more help is found. They are running out of essential supplies and it would be helpful if Steve went over to the wholesalers to pick up more.

The equipment recently bought is still being evaluated to see if it would be of use.

Now that it is fine to make a noise, he heads to the wet room to shower and shave. The shower automatically shoots jets of body lotion treated hot water all around his body when he steps into the cubicle. This quickly refreshes him to be ready to commence his day properly. He is a night owl and only comes alive when nine to five workers have already headed home. His attire changes to become the norm for the neighbourhood: artisan and organic, the appropriate uniform of a green warrior or easy going liberal by wearing colourful long-sleeved cotton tops, strong hard wearing bright jeans complimented in winter by a thick patterned woollen jumper and a well-stitched woollen jacket. His favourite denim boots remain on his feet.

Their household routines are well established and done automatically without any debate. In the evening, after eating together, Mi-Cha tidy ups and performs other housekeeping duties like sorting out clothes for the nightly wash, then heads to the bedroom at around seven to rest for a couple of hours before her next working stunt. Steve checks to ensure that he has enough loose tobacco, papers and cannabis resin to make several joints prior to heading out the door to get out of her way. They generally get together again in bed when he returns home around two in the morning. For different reasons, both are tired and soon fall asleep wrapped up in separate custom-made duvets on a king size luxury soft leather bed with a matching ottoman. In the morning, Mi-Cha rises first around eight, picks up any discarded clothing, empties the washing machine and hangs up the cleaned clothing in the utility room, then heads out the house for her morning jog and stretch exercises in the local park. Stretches based on a mix of Yoga, Pilates, Tia Chi and Taekwondo warm-up routines. A slow jogging pace is gradually increased to get the blood and heat flowing through her body before stopping at her favourite spot to spend thirty minutes going through her routine of pulling her back and limbs in a rhythmic and well-practiced manner. The chosen spot is a small nock of grass surrounded by tall sycamores and maples. Dog walkers like to stop and watch her performance while their dogs do their business. Steve insists that she stays in trim and the sexual activity that occurs when she comes back is more like a perfunctory inspection of her toned body and testing of sensual sensitivity than lovemaking. He wants her to keep her body flexible and agile to be able to comfortably bend her limbs and tighten her muscles. The daily inspection ends with a shared shower. Afterwards, Mi-Cha disappears to the back room for the rest of the day. Steve tends to spend the mornings in his dressing gown relaxing over an extended breakfast, drinking loads of tea and munching toast spread thick with marmite, sometimes adding strong favoured cheese and Worcester sauce to give it more kick. The remains of a fruit salad, usually prepared earlier by Mi-Cha when she created muesli for herself, provide some other necessary vitamins and minerals. He only listens to a jazz music radio channel, as he hates the noise of animated commentators broadcasting their opinions on the latest news or the wailing of sycophantic daytime music presenters polluting the airwaves. He is not really bothered about being out of date with the latest political debate. He knows that he can just join in at any time by expressing views that are expected of him. The only information absorbed is the gossip in the morning's tabloid that Mi-Cha brings back after exercising.

This councillor rarely gets out of his robe before midday. Any council work that requires his physical presence normally occurs late afternoon at the earliest and chores that require him to jump in the black Cherokee jeep to go out to the supermarket or wholesalers can wait until after lunchtime when the traffic is quieter again. No point queuing when you do not have to. Mi-Cha has her own car, a sporty silver Alfa Romeo, which inevitably Steve uses more than she does. None of his extensive leisure time is spent on pursuing an interest in creative art. He has long ago put aside his paintbrush and accepted a sedentary lifestyle. His passion for the up town art scene had subsided and he is no longer a dedicated follower of it. Any pretended love for modern art with its emphasis on combining all the mediums to show the dynamics and interplay of form, language, music and texture long forgotten as any great work that ever came out of it has already been re-used by brand creation consultants or hidden away by the rich looking for an investment which will protect their wealth. Art is now just a commodity within the creative economy where artists promote their own image. Instead, he is now genuinely enjoying the fruits of his labour, which considering his lack of formal qualifications and personal effort is remarkable.

BECOMING A COUNCILLOR

Steve drifted into local politics when the sight of Julia first attracted his eye one night in the Captain's Retreat pub. He spotted her sitting at a table waiting for other party members before heading upstairs to a private function room. It was a group of environmental activists having a fortnightly get together and he instinctively recognised vulnerability in her character that others never saw. They perceived a confident organiser with strong feminist views who knew how to articulate her concerns, a natural leader of the local environmental party due to her strong Friends of the Earth credentials. He saw someone looking for approval and affirmation for her right to be there: blue-eyed Julia, mid-twenties, hazel blond hair, with a slender figure, easy on the eye and definitely alluring if dressed appropriately.

As this opportunist knew nothing about their concerns for the environment or their policies, his initial approach to joining the company of these local activists just appeared sinister and at the same time infantile, but his persistence paid off and he endeared himself as the group gradually accepted him as a possible willing foot soldier when campaigning.

Steve's was oblivious to their initial feelings of aversion towards him while he thought they were a bunch of cranks looking for something to do during the middle of the week: exhibitionists looking for a cause to follow.

The activists also believed he would be a good thermometer for judging public opinion. His lack of knowledge concerning issues of the day signalled recognition on their part of the failure to get their message across to the common man. It was no good intellectuals like them prevaricating change if the masses failed to understand. The local group had enthusiastic members from the revamped old town but it could not be said that they truly represented the mainstream in the town, as there was a lack of membership from the adjacent quiet dormitories. The presence of only a young vegetarian six-form schoolgirl dragging her randy boyfriend reluctantly in toll both testified this view. This local group had about twenty fully committed members, which may sound low, was, in fact, comparable to the numbers in the local mainstream parties. It was just a fact that only a few people participated in the turning of the wheels of democracy.

Simon was the closest member of the group to Julia. He was a tall confident person who could argue any justification for his actions, a man who came across as someone who never had to struggle for anything in his life. Steve made sure he won Simon's approval by keeping on his best side. This perceived adversary was passionate about moving society away from cornucopian consumption attitudes and Promethean

leanings to manipulate world resources by blindly
accepting the fallacy that continual economic growth
was imperative. The conservative established view of
the past was by its nature romanticised, an unreal
depiction. It's adherence to rationality and scientific
progress had descended into valueless materialism
and self-absorption. It was imperative a different way
of thinking and communicating be promoted to
separate future man from past follies.

The latest recruit's willingness to be an active
member did have its limits, he always made sure he
was not available for bee counting surveys, conserving
South Downs nature trails or any other sort of feel-
good events. Attending meetings held in pubs or going
back to someone's house for a few smokes was the
only physical involvement that appealed to him.
Nevertheless, by playing the sycophant he gained a
foothold and was eventually welcomed into the inner
sanctum.

The main concern of the group was always
sustainability and the need to save the planet.
Debates about green energy were circular in nature.
The cost of it increased the levels of fuel poverty and
premature deaths in the poorer communities but it
was justified because all countries had to do their bit
and make sacrifices. Africa should not bear all the
pain. Although the stopping of carbon burning and
nuclear energy generation here would not slow down
climate change it would encourage the developing
world to adopt friendlier energy policies. In the
meantime, other countries cheap energy policies, that
allowed them to manufacture cheaper goods to sell in

this country, had to be tolerated despite contributing to the creation of a poorer menial underclass at home, which again contributed to premature deaths. Anyway, once they gained the reins of power all spending on armaments would stop, freeing up money to subsidise heating, especially in the colder north. Steve pointed out that there were bad people in this world and the country had to protect itself. The retort from the extreme element of the group was the policies of the West that made them bad. Once the world sees that we were in it together then aggression would stop. Our enemies shall be turned into friends. It was clear to them that Steve just did not understand the big picture. In the meantime, a particularly cold winter and energy blackouts would be tantamount to murder for the northern poor.

As for Steve, their meetings were like being in a medical ward for the mentally insane as their self-importance and self-righteousness allowed them to ignore the obvious fact that the rest of the world held different stances. People demanded hassle free convenient living with the availability of cheap food, reliable energy and affordable global travel. People nowadays particularly resented any interference from nature. For modern man nature was only something to marvel and watch on television. The desire to change business, social and private practices to accommodate nature required drastic measures, with the culling of humanity a top priority. The poor knew by instinct that it would be them who suffered and not the self-chosen elites. The group also did not understand how society really worked. They had no idea of the petty rivalries that existed within the different communities. The most intransigent people could be well paid blue-collar workers or self-employed who handled money, not the rich. These people continually compared themselves with childhood acquaintances that they left behind and assume to be living off the state as they spend all their life earning money.

In the early days, he did not like the late-night drinking and smoking sessions either as talk always led to dry debates centred on Simon's view of the world. The environmentalists would sort out the national debt. Major parties deliberately ran with a fiscal deficit as they saw it as political suicide to leave anything in the exchequer for the opposition to claim as their own. It has been a long time since all the major parties adopted a two-tier socio-economic system to allow the country to survive in an extremely competitive world. So, there was just one more step required without the need of double think indoctrination to get all the public to understand less was good, as they knew consumerism had to be curtailed to save the planet. Away from politics, Simon was particularly interested in up town contemporary culture. To Simon, up town was the international home of contemporary art, a community vastly inflated by home-grown and international talent. The rest of the world was only a few hours away by plane or in instant contact by phone or Wi-Fi communications. It drew artists towards it to do original, challenging and exciting things. Its art reflected the fluidity of the place as its artists' sense of being came from the global community and was not influenced by local historic or regional boundaries.

Contemporary art was on display and available to buy
everywhere, an art reflecting the internationalisation
of the place and its divergence from the rest of the
country. Collages of photographs, paint, chalk, and
man make or organic materials glued or screwed
together. These works showcased alongside video
productions of sound, dialogue, movement; all meant
to deliberately send conflicting information to the
senses. The use of different media signalled the end of
boundaries, narrow thinking, promoting the
acceptance of a multicultural one-world village.
Decomposing or unravelling elements within the
structures symbolised the precipitous and unstable
relationship of western man and his dialectics with
other cultures, the environment and the natural
world. The intentional superficiality seen in modern
art was a reaction against the denigration of the
importance of art as a significant cultural
contribution to life in postmodernity.

These types of accolades could continue all night. The
continual bumming up of the up town scene was
excruciatingly boring. Many great western countries
laid claim to be the centre of contemporary art, while
other regions in this country had magnificent teaching
institutions. The core message was always the same.
Art enriched lives and contemporary art in this
country was the best medium for explaining life in an
artificially constructed world. Steve was usually
sound asleep on a comfortable couch by the time
Simon had finished his rhetoric. He had been
listening to such well-meaning interpretation of art
all his life and it always bored him. For him, it was
always a bit of fun and a chance to meet other fun-

loving people. In addition, he knew from experience it was a day job to pay the bills. Today, it is a numbers game as institutions seek students and sponsorship to supply the demand to rush people through the doors to create a simplistic and easily digestible culture for a populist market.

Anyway, to be close to Julia, he endured it all. The end justified the means and he was just as stubborn in his mission as they were in theirs. In addition, his previous alternative lifestyles as a Wicca convert; an artist and a peasant farmer enhanced his credibility. On paper, these alternative backgrounds, however shortly lived, were probably more apt for the acceptance of a green dominated future than the backgrounds of some of the more illustrious members in the local group. The main qualifications for some of these members were being avid readers of the Guardian and the Independent or purely perceiving themselves as being worldlier wise.

At that time, Julia was the only real standout to contest a seat in the up and coming local council elections. Yet, the revamped old town covered two possible winnable wards so the infighting for the remaining seat was fierce. When his support was confidentially sought, Steve naturally agreed in the right of that faction to choose the representative for the other contested seat. He even played the role of arbiter trying to bring all the factions together for the common good. Helping to defuse discord between rivals, reminding everyone that labels should not be attached to people and they were a collegial party with a common aim. This all meant that no one saw him as a threat. The gay faction eventually got the upper hand over a small but vocal lesbian and transgender contingent. The chosen candidate was a plum early retired university professor of archaeology sporting a grey goatee beard with flowing long hair tied at the back into a ponytail, a product of two Cambridge alumni. He grew up in a time when revolution became a commodity for the walls of students and the songs of pop stars. His wolfish eyes suggested that there was still a lot of life in the old dog and that his sexual encounter headcount was not over yet.

All seemed to be going well for the party as Julia and the other representative gathered a lot of local public backing from the electorate in the lead up to the formal announcement for candidacies. This left the traditional parties resigned to their fate in these wards. At least none of these parties would be losing ground on each other but it did suggest that a minority run council was on the cards. Then an unfortunate event for democracy but a fortuitous one for Steve pushed him to the fore, giving him his unexpected role in frontline politics. At an open meeting held at an old folk's home to rally support while partaking in tea and cakes, things started to unravel for the gay candidate. His legal life partner had received an anonymous tipoff that he was the injured party of a behind his back affair between his partner and the party's campaign manager for the up and coming elections, and that the adulterous pair did not disguise their relationship. The innocent injured party, a natural homemaker, by nature more feminine in manner and emotion, fortified by downing several large glasses of gin, took himself off to this meeting to see for himself if there was any truth in these allegations. He knew that his partner had picked a profession and interests that kept him in close proximity to available young males. He had previously wondered if the nights away from home were really work or political campaigning related. He knew the *modus operandi* of his partner, as he was once the desirable young lover that led to the abandonment of a previous partner. The big difference now is that he had the legal right to sue for every penny going. This adamantine bride was going to curtail the amorous plans of the two-timing shit.

The result was a carry-on film type fiasco that some national news organisations would later give coverage under the heading cupcake fight at the old folks' corral, reporting that shocked pensioners watched on as obscenities and savoury dishes of all kinds hurled across the hall. When the disgruntled lover arrived, the meeting had just started with his partner about to open his address. Julia and the rest of the environmental delegation sat neatly behind him. The injured party quickly saw a younger version of himself a few feet behind the guest speaker and immediately picked up unsaid signals, which initiated the launch of a verbal attack on his life partner and the new love interest while the accuser walked down the central aisle towards them. Julia who made herself pleasant quickly resolved these early exchanges without appearing biased to either party who now stood five to six feet apart. Unfortunately, the truce did not last long and all hell soon broke out when ill-advised words passed between both sides.

Some of the pensioners sensed the coming spectacle and drew up their seats close, in anticipation of a day to remember instead of a day duller than normal when the visit of local candidates was first announced. The tears and tantrums came when the injured party reacted to gloating and the loathing in the facial expressions of the accused lovers. Tears ran continuously down his cheeks as the councillor elect's lover gained courage and retorted to the earlier outburst by saying that the legal partner of the candidate was a bastard of a whore and a two-timing tart who would go up the back alley with anyone, and that the prospective councillor deserved better. A cup of tea was grabbed from a nearby table and its contents accurately thrown into the face of this foulmouthed cow, the injured party's actions and words. The standard son of a bitch reply instantly herald open conflict as cakes and other assortments flew between and over Julia, who intelligently jumped out of the way to let the winner to be decided by brute force. Politics was going to have to take second place to the affairs of the heart. The pensioners held their position while speedily munching away at their sandwiches to stop them from being used as impromptu missiles. The candidate at the centre of this dispute followed Julia's example and sharply got out of the firing zone.

As the verbal slagging and food throwing continued it was met with approval, laughter and encouragement for more direct action. Pensioners who moments earlier were stalling or absolutely refusing to be taken into the makeshift auditorium which normally served as the communal area and dining room, suddenly found the enthusiasm and energy to rush into the meeting, causing chaos at the entrance door. Discarded Zimmer frames tripping up unsuspecting new arrivals pushed forwarded by the impatient crowd backing up behind them. The catcalls of you bitch and you cow, and the external encouragement corralled the combatants closer together until they were within touching distance. The councillor elect's lover picked up a pot of tea and poured the contents over the other's head. The old folk were now having a wonderful time and mainly supported the injured party because he had lost his man. The only thing missing were trays of custard pies to give the combatants supplies of clown-like ammunition. In addition, private fights were breaking out all over the auditorium as vendettas and acts of revenge for previous grudges were carried out. Old Mavis was seen smacking cankerous Fred across the face when he complained that her heckling was drowning out the shouts of the love rivals. Fred was the notorious arse pincher in this old folk's home.

The fighting commenced properly when the injured party leaped at the throat of his love rival and began to strangle him. The lover's response was to scratch the face of the other and spit into his eyes causing the first signs of blood, which raised everyone's fervour. The spilling of blood was soon shared when the campaign manager's studded earring was ripped off. The home's concierge half-heartedly intervened by telling them to behave themselves and to act like men. However, the jeers of the crowd dissuaded him to push his intervention any further. The combatants by this time were wrestling at close quarters. In the melee, arms were being bent, genitals mangled and clothing torn. Blood and squashed food smeared the floor causing the pair to slip and slide. They were fighting over an old rascal like two demented banshees.

The concierge finally pulled himself away from the fun to call the police. Somehow, the press found out as well. By the time, the police arrived to break up the catfight, the local press were already in place taking snapshots and filming the bloodied and dishevelled combatants, who were rolling on the floor. Each enjoyed a brief moment of dominance by gaining the top spot where the other's hair could be pulled and the face scratched in any remaining untouched part as the head was banged against the floor. The prospective councillor for the ward now just sat in a corner with his head lowered in his hands, as Julia patted him on the back offering all the sympathy in the world as his hoped political career went down the pan. Subsequently, he would just disappear as if the ground opened up and swallowed him. With only a short time to decide, another candidate for the coming elections had to be found. The lesbian faction reconfirmed its desire to put forward one of its members. Julia pointed out that a man should be selected, as having only female candidates was not a democratic or fair representation of the local party's demographic. After all, they stood for social justice for all. The lesbians were not happy with this turn of events but reluctantly agreed to allow a male to be put forward to the electorate. Following democratic practices had worked against them and some of them thought they had should have held out, as there was merit in enforcing your views on the rest of the world.

It was also pointed out that the representative's background should reflect the mores of mainstream society so maybe a heterosexual male would complement the feminist viewpoint. It would help the cause even further if he had some business experience, having knowledge of the pros and cons experienced by the small businessperson in the wards, in particular, of arts and craft merchandise. So being the only male acceptable to everyone, as they believed he could be manipulated unlike a big fish like Simon, resulted in Steve's recommendation as the other candidate. The gay faction were in disorder due to the altercation at the old folk's home and in its current turmoil did not put up any resistance to this nomination. Julia also was coming around to the view that it would not be a bad thing to have a fellow party councillor happy to be subordinate to her.

Steve duly won the seat, a seat in a trendy ward that, of course, a dead sheep would have won if a green sash were put on it. As it turned out Steve was acceptable to everyone in the council as well. Being apolitical, open to friendly advice and always looking for personal gain, he was naturally sociable to everyone and never acrimonious. It was obvious that this new councillor did not intend to rock the boat, whistle blow on corrupt archaic practices or recommend efficiencies and radical changes. Unaccustomed as he was to the trappings of power his easily inflated ego soon adjusted to it as he became suitably pompous. He embraced the pantomime and played his expected part in it. Councillors of all parties were happy to converse with him in the corridors of power, be that only the town hall.

Julia was happy as well, as he initially did what he was told and followed the party line when it came to voting. His full-time assistant was also happy. Left to work alone at her own pace to make autonomous decisions suited her personality better than if she were constantly under scrutiny. PR trainers from central office gave him private tuition on the usage, at appropriate times, of an array of glib phrases and attention catching words; instructions on how to handle the media to get your message across. They reminded him that the objective was to direct the opinion of the public and never condemn or label them as that would put off their targeted audience. Publicity stunts must always be authorised by central office while the mission statement repeated as often as possible: *the party was large enough to cope and run for higher office but small enough to care and never forget its core values.*

When he was canvassing for votes, the electorate thought he would make a wonderful councillor. The fact that he never used local amenities or experienced the endeavours required to make a community business successful did not prevent him from appearing the part. He had seen enough headlines in the tabloids to know what fears all communities perceived. When addressing the old or young mothers he promised better amenities. He told local businesses that green did not mean more bureaucracy. He easily won the pub drinkers' vote. The well-to-do vote did not require reassurance about cleaner streets or wellbeing issues, as they already possessed the accoutrements that wealth brings. If anything desired was not found in town, they would simply jump into their 4x4s to find it, whether that was in nearby towns or up town. Instead, he spoke to them about the need to do their little bit to save the planet and to help the suffering poor Africans.

The representative of the Morley ward was in no danger of losing motivation, passion or interest, as he never had any of these attitudes in the first place. He sometimes made a *faux pas* by nodding at the wrong time or mistakenly associating someone with something not linked to them. However, nothing controversial was said, as he never chatted about disputed issues. He was more likely only to get someone's favourite football team mixed up. Predictably, his quick humour and unabashed attitude usually got him out of trouble. He did what was expected of him, which was not much, especially when he found out that there was no legal requirement to force him to attend general council meetings or be available to sit on committees. He could vanish from the public eye when required as the official part-time nature of the role gave a ready-made excuse for his unavailability due to urgent private matters. He did participate when he found out if there were rewards on offer. When pre-warned, he did make an effort to attend local planning permission sessions if a grateful citizen required a desirable outcome. He found it good practice to help people who promised to be kind to him. In addition, he automatically got unexpected allowances by accepting to be nominated as a paid non-executive board member on rarely convened public bodies, as well as invites to extended trips to twinned cities in Spain and Italy, and as a representative of the electorate there were invites to local galas and diners.

Overall being a councillor did not interfere with his other commitments. As a night person, his social activities were not unduly affected; any drunkenness or other potentially damaging antic was out of sight of the well wrapped up in bed good honest folk. Sometimes attending to council affairs was the only reason why he had to get out of bed. Only the electorate could remove him from office and the next election was still too far in the future to worry too much about it. On the streets, his ever-present smile and tactile mannerisms made him approachable. The general opinion was that he was down to earth and amiable. The public liked him, as he always stopped and listened to their concerns. He became a well-known man in his ward. The fact was these concerns never perturbed him as they went in one ear and immediately out the other.

Secure in the knowledge of Mi-Cha's unquestioning obedience and the kudos obtained from being elected into public office, Steve advanced his plans on attaining Julia. Good progress was quickly made as he displaced Simon as her second in command and political confidant. This was only natural as some council business had to be kept in-house. Steve always had a willing ear as Julia enjoyed the coaching and supervisory roles in their emerging relationship. Steve's immunity from open criticism inevitably increased as his standing with Julia became stronger.

He was only ever admonished when he let her down during council debates when his contribution would have swung the decision. His unreliability was an issue but was never addressed head on and in the end condoned as just a part of who he was. Internal party member complaints about his lack of serious involvement fell on deaf ears, simply dismissed as jealous malcontent murmurings. From the outside, it would look strange but within the whirlpool of daily political life, his behaviour and lack of real commitment were eventually seen as normal, just typical Steve.

Simon grew more frustrated with the local group as he resented his diminishing influence on it. In the end, he picked up sticks to join a larger branch of the party down the coast, stating that the town was too small a backwater to attract the attention of the big boys up-town; if he wanted to progress he had to become more visible to the party elites.

THE LABOURS OF RUTH

Some children when they have grown up in a loveless or troubled home search for emotional warmth in adulthood, others, like Steve, have no need to thrive by bathing in this type of heat. He never went through the growing pains of confused emotions, no turmoil and no love felt or given. He would never hold any strong self-reinforcing beliefs; never consider contemplating a different way of life to alter his ego to achieve any form of enlightenment to negate his natural selfishness or to embrace any form of compassion. He was purely and simply animalistic, soulless. The end would always justify the means, so long as the end suited him. Women did not have to worry if he would love them tomorrow as he never loved them from the start. There would be no love-hate craze or competing for their affections. Although never to enter into a deeply intimate relationship, women would be a source of entertainment, amusement, adventure, and income, a challenge that was happily accepted. He could never be a lone wolf. The support of women was required to provide the domestic comforts that he needed. The women in his life would always have to make the compromises and sacrifices, as he did what he pleased without any moral or social inhibitions imposed upon him. This included reacting to any sexual impulse that expressed itself.

Steve's parents both originally came from the east end of up town. They moved out to Railhead when an opportunity to start up a private security guard concern materialised for his father. It was not an enterprise guaranteed to bring huge financial reward but it meant being free to make his own decisions, to stand on his own feet. The family established itself in the north of the town while his father initially made a success of his newfound independence, winning small contracts to check and protect private and public premises. In the eyes of a child, everything appeared regular and consistent, an early childhood spent without serious illness or violent disputes between parents that he could remember. His parents managed to reasonably quickly repay the mortgage for their terrace house and Steve was a model student at junior school, succeeding in winning a scholarship to a Jesuit school in the area.

Unfortunately, a longer than expected recession along with changing work practices curtailed most of his father's opportunities, at a time when big national competitors started to undercut small firms by being able to invest in technology and by employing aggressive accountancy practices to reduce overheads. Quite simply his father did not have the aptitude or means to learn new skills or deploy technology required to compete. In the end, to keep afloat he had to accept subcontract work from these nationals at much reduced rates. Eventually, he lost all motivation and drifted into alcoholism. At home, there was no more show of kindly warmth between father, mother and child, only apprehension as any small incident could spark a violent reaction from the drunken husband. His mother used to wait, watching the door with her dark swollen eyes when she heard a key turning the lock; forever trapped in a confined space, isolated, isolated in a marriage formed by following conventions that pressured the young to pair up to bear children. As a young teenager, Steve had nothing of his own. At Christmas, his father would sometimes give him well-wrapped presents of empty boxes just to see the expression on his face. Most nights coming home from school meant seeing a dad drunk on the couch, mum sulking in her corner and nothing cooked for tea. Consequently, he had to become streetwise and a bit of a survivalist. He was more than happy to move away from the parental home when the first opportunity presented itself.

School friends became his effective family. His small nucleus of friends included Jason and Martin. Jason, Martin, and Steve were three young men, all roughly the same age and from the same social class; united as friends not due to having the same temperament, hobbies or similar childhood experiences but by having the common desire to escape to another existence. Jason was the most cerebral of the gang, the teacher's pet attracting special attention from father McDermott who seemed to have seen him as a possible recruit to the faith. Steve was a rule breaker, a chancer. Martin was the most down to earth character, a practical-minded person with the physical strength to get things done. When they left school, Jason and Steve would pursue art studies together. Martin was not interested in art and started to disappear on his own. He travelled months on end on the continent on his motorbike, initially struggling but finally succeeding to make new friends abroad.

Later, some young northerners attracted by the promise of a professional career in engineering arrived on the scene. It was a time when leaving home was a complete break from family. A time when not only were countries insular places but discrimination based on regional differences was ripe. Leaving home then was an adventure into the unknown. In their case to become cheap labour for the rapidly expanding electronic industries. It was a time when professionalism was being redefined with engineers downgraded to be considered as skilful blue-collar workers. Instead of associating their position with its Latin root of genius, the English association with engine, a mechanical device, was now applied. Several months after arriving in the South they not only found the cost of living to be prohibitive but that their wage was relatively unsubstantial; a well-tipped local milkman doing his morning float run earned more than they did. However, compared to the cash-strapped young men from Railhead the northerners were like rich free spenders, manna from heaven.

There was nothing clever or devious about Steve's behaviour during his teenage years. He was no smart pickup artist, no sex god, or one of the beautiful people who would be automatically welcomed anywhere. There was no thought-out intentness of purpose in his actions. In many ways, he was just happy-go-lucky with an extravert's approach to everything, a doer regardless of the outcome, not a pontificator; good fun in any company when there was plenty of money to go around; daring and barefaced by nature because he could not delineate between right or wrong. When others picked up the bills and the consequences then life was easy to navigate, stress-free and so good for the health. Because he did not experience any serious deterrents in his early years to dissuade him otherwise, this carefree attitude would stay with him throughout his life. The absence of any form of neuroticism meant he did not perceive threats or dangers, which could have altered his behaviour. People dismissed him as a serious risk to their way of life or ambitions by wrongly assuming he played by their rules. It did not matter what part of society they came from they all had a code to follow or life within it would be impossible. Whereas, Steve's rules remained steadfast and never progressed beyond those developed in the playground where strength was might. A world where not backing down and stubbornly pursuing your prey were great attributes.

The son resembled his father physically and in many ways in character. The only difference was bad luck would not dog him. His morale would never suffer from having to work hard just to see the effort fail. In fact, due to the indifference of authority to minor law breaking so long as an insignificant minority indulged in it, he would always capitalize on his selfish misdemeanours. He also had the advantage of never attempting to engage in the world of work, which might have exposed weaknesses in his ability to learn new skills or exposed him to years of drudgery or chronic stress conditions. Consequently, his nerves and ego never paid a price for years of obligation to remain focused on the pursuit to put food on the table by working for an employer; never having to knuckle down when your heart implored you to walk away or to suffer the penalties of overworking. There was no need to change his mannerisms to keep in with management or customers. Instead, he became a good observer of others as they rushed about in their daily lives. He would forever have the same simplistic opinion of ordinary people as those in the top echelons of society: they were only resources to use. This enabled him to have no prejudices, as a resource was just a resource no matter its origin. Shielding from self-doubt or remorse gave him an unblemished perception of himself. He could smell out women to exploit. This was not due to an inherent psychological ability to judge people but merely an instinctive blunderbuss attitude, which by its very nature eventually allowed him to meet women who appeared in control of their lives but in truth lived a sham existence where fears, insecurities and anxieties lay below the surface.

Steve's gregarious nature led him up town where he joined an artist commune sponsored by a left-wing council. Around thirty artists shared amenities and produced works for public spaces about the borough. Instead of promoting intellectual or artistic excellence, the commune was to communicate the emotional state of the nation, not joy or happiness but despair and anger. Steve called it his red period. He had no formal qualifications as he had dropped out of his art course several years earlier, only natural brag to produce primitive and freely expressed works, which suited the philosophy of the council, as it appeared to give power to the people by letting the masses release their creativeness. In his paintings shape, brushstroke and colour rarely reflected strength or vigour, solidity or fluidity, violence or tranquillity. Scale and size did not purposely exaggerate man's place in the world or reflect unbalanced relationships. There was no hidden message in the number and types of colour used to convey mood. No unassuming Lowry-esque depictions of urban, land or seascapes. He merely painted the same type of images regardless of the intended destination for the finished product. Experience did lead to improvement in his application but it remained messy and inexplicable with only the name of the painting giving any clue to its meaning.

Frolicking, dope and late-night drinking summed up these years, all at the ratepayers' expense while at the same time claiming all the benefits going. Anything illegal accepted as a way of life attributed to natural rebellion against a perceived aggressive authoritarian regime. Counterfeit banknotes flooded the drinking hostels were this commune drank. By skipping fares, Steve never paid for travel around town. It was then that Steve met his future wife Ruth, who was a few years older than him, at one of the open parties at the council owned studios. She worked in the city where one of her adventurous female colleagues encouraged her to attend a soiree there. Both had jobs that were reasonably well paid, secure but essentially dull. This colleague convinced her that it would be a hoot as these nights had a reputation for being fun and off the wall. Simply put, if not on the top shelf regarding looks, women seeking men tend to have to take greater risks to find easy sex. In this case, Ruth was a bit plump with thick uncontrollable hair. She was an orphan who came into some money at the age of twenty-one. Insecurities while growing up without parents made her an ideal companion for Steve. It did not take long for him to attach his sails to her ship and redirect her in a direction she would not have ever assumed to take, to become his angel with big tits. After knowing each other for only a couple of months they married.

Soon afterwards this period, Steve would disappear for weeks on end to Florence to visit an ex-arts teacher that both Jason and he knew. Jason would inevitably always be in residence in the villa located within a couple of acres of olive tree inhabited land. The former teacher was living the good life by creating his own little commune for friends and invited art students. It was a fun place to spend time; liberal thinking girls came and went, taking advantage of a free holiday in exchange for being jolly. Steve would test how far their willingness to be entertaining would go. Experimentation in all types of sexual perversion occurred, mainly for shock value than real seriousness to experiment. Guests got used to the sight of Steve masturbating with melons and attempting strangulation to heighten arousal. Even the latest girlfriend of the owner of the villa was not immune from his sexual advances. Jason fell out with him when he persuaded two passing through Polish girls to share his bed. Jason had taken a likening to one of them but after this episode just referred to them as dirty cows.

The only downside to life in Tuscany was the eternally long debates on art theory, in particular, the Renaissance. It was essentially a student commune so debate was not a surprising event nonetheless the pretentiousness of so-called experts was overbearing. More so as Steve knew the protagonists were just piss heads like him. Their hyperboles had more to do with the influence of hallucinogens then honest heart-felt beliefs. However, it gave him a taste for Italian life, wetting his appetite for something more substantial.

Steve would also stop over at Martin's new abode in Burgundy near Mâcon just off the A6 AutoRoute when travelling back and forth. It was a convenient stopping point on his long journey. Martin had moved to this area recently after a financially crippling divorce from his German wife. He bought a detached house within one acre of land, outside Mâcon, where he managed to get some part-time employment in the postal service. It was previously a family home and the remnants of the activity of young children were still visible. There was a protected outdoor playpen in a large garden containing vegetable and fruit plots. The previous owner had kept a sheep that doubled as a family pet to keep the grass short. Classifying it as livestock allowed the claiming of livestock rebates. Martin kept up the same arrangement after the previous owner explained the setup. An oddity of the place was a dug hole fenced off with a low-lying length of rope. Fish caught in the Saône were thrown into it, left to mature, and ate when the family fancied some fish. A hose of running water maintained the water level and helped to oxygenise it. Considering there had been kids running around, it seemed an unsafe arrangement.

As usual, Martin was a good host. He had stocked up the house with booze of all types. His appearance showed the tell-tale sign of a man stuck in a rut with alcohol as his constant companion, a deep crimson nose protruded from an unkempt face. He was freefalling as he waited for his self-esteem to kick in and demand action to reclaim his life and to climb up the social ladder again. The stopovers gave the friends only enough time to wander into the village for a drink then return to the house to listen to old favourite songs while talking about the old days or discussing plans. As it was with friends, one was in a good place at these moments in time and the other struggling to decide his next step. Steve was ecstatic about the possibilities of shipping back Italian goods to sell; in particular, the mark up in quality Hi-Fi and coffee making equipment would be very rewarding. Martin was not in the best of places concerning his mental and physical shape, he could go one way or the other depending on his behaviour and decisions over the next few years. He had spent literally a decade of his life working long night shifts to acquire wealth only to see most of it torn away from him. He was going stir crazy due to this self-imposed prolonged incarceration away from anyone he knew. Nevertheless, he did not want to talk to anyone about his concerns, his only desire was to be left alone to work things out. Breathing space to determine the next path to take, a path that could affect his wellbeing for the rest of his life. He was also reluctant to go back to old milieus due to fallouts with his family. All this produced the feelings of failure conjured up with the idea of going backwards in his life rather than forward. It was a case of staying put until motivated to move on. The big question was did he have any motivation left to resume a life of hard time-consuming work after believing he had left it all behind him. He felt that time was against him and that he would only have one more chance to succeed again. Failure to re-engage in the workplace could sink him.

Eventually, after many hedonistic visits to Florence with financially rewarding returns home thanks to the foreseen profits obtained by selling desirable upmarket products, Steve decided to convince Ruth to move out permanently to Italy to start life afresh. She did not take much persuasion as her mood reflected that of the country at this time. In her case, she was waning towards depression because her working routine had stagnated. She agreed to pack in her job, sell up and gamble on a better life abroad where good weather was guaranteed. She left the decision on where they would live to Steve. Her only proviso was it had to be nice and homely. This gave Steve the opportunity to travel all over the Italian mainland in a second-hand Range Rover before deciding on a small hold farm south of Naples, which was several hours drive away. It suited their budget and complied with Steve's idea of rustic living. It was a hard to get to remote habitation perching on the side of a steep wooded hill. Any vehicle had to first climb to the summit then make its way down a tricky track until it

could go no further. Traces of an ancient forest
remained in little clusters near the summit of the
hills, with truffle oak, chestnut, flowering ash, white
poplar continuing to survive. Further down the slopes
olive and carob dominated the landscape. The
property had been derelict for years, had become
squalid and required major work to make it fit for
human habitation. Around the house old vines laid
uncultivated in their rows. The locale was peopled
with ageing inhabitants, ecstatic about a young couple
moving back to the area, regardless if they were
Italian or not.

They left the modern secular world behind to enter a
world without conveniences, a world harder on the
women than the men, a world where water and
electricity were not in constant limitless supply. They
now had to be managed. Ruth left behind cupboards
full of coats, skirts, blouses and shoes for a life of
wearing sensible boots and baggy clothing to allow
free movement to do her labours. She had no more
need for drawers full of makeup, cleansers and the
likes. To her surprise, the climate was not remarkably
warmer, only more settled, dry and less windy. The
most noticeable differences being reliable summer
heat, the absence of morning ground frost or chilly
days in winter, with daylight hours significantly less
dependent on the seasons. It was the different terrain
and the people that made the greatest impact on her
than anything else. The farmhouse was a modest two
floor stone built box with small entrances and narrow
windows. They had to learn to duck their heads
instinctively to pass under the low lintels of the doors.
A raised level terrace gave access to a potentially

comfortable outdoor seating area. The sun bathed this patio in the morning as it travelled westward behind the summit of their hill.

The world of consumerism was a long way away while TV and radio receptions were poor. There was no running tap water or inside sanitation. The toilet was a shed placed over a cesspit. An open water barrel collected rainwater. In times of drought, they would have to collect water from an underground spring further down the slope. Bathing could be restricted to a wipe down with a damp cloth. A diesel generator produced electricity. Mains electricity only reached the nearby village where a branch line connected it to the national grid several miles away. The village was situated in the heart of the valley and along the sides of the hills with a population of several hundred living in dilapidated splendour in family houses that were now too large to be maintained by mostly aging residents. House chores in this environment took longer and were physically demanding, hard on a woman not use to labour. To keep dust under control required continual brushing of floors and wiping down of furniture. Washing clothes meant scrubbing them by hand and then continually re-rinsing them to ensure removal of soapsuds, stains and dirt. On the plus side, there was no shortage of wood to burn for heat or cooking.

In the city, man created his own work, whereas the terrain dictated countryside life. Here, arduous conditions demanded cooperation. The harshness of life also created strong familial bonds with a natural distrust of authority. It was a time-consuming subsistence farming lifestyle where neighbours helped each other. The rock-strewn hilly terrain limited the yield of the harvest and only large subsidies allowed farming to be viable. Local cooperatives pressed and marketed harvested grapes, citrus fruit and olives. Following traditional methods, each member of the cooperative could turn surplus grapes into homemade wine and grappa, served in thick stoneware jugs. Neighbours were a great source of help as they provided the couple with sound guidance on the buying of livestock to provide eggs and meat. Others taught Steve how to hunt for wild sources of meat in the adjoining hills. Hunting etiquette and the safe use of firearms passed on to him by supervising him out in the woods. Ruth was shown how to cook local recipes like rabbit with sorrel. If she did not cook then they would go hungry.

Sunday was a time for sociability. After the church service, men sat in bars as the women prepared lunch. Language expressed in their faces and hands, as many different bodily and facial expressions could signify yes, no or doubt. The survivors of this terrain had a modest existence, lived off the land, held uncomplicated values and truths, and lived very long rewarding active lives; this longevity was passed on to their descendants. The needy found a second family in the Church. The Church in the south had a tradition of rescuing orphans and abandoned children to teach them the skills required to maintain its magnificence; this produced the alchemists, scribes, carpenters, stonemasons, sculptors, painters and musical composers that drove technical and artistic advancement in the Middles Ages onwards.

On top of everything, and with their limited
knowledge of the language and customs, the married
couple had a house to renovate and had to establish
official residency. All compounded by the fact that the
local dialect was distinctly different from the textbook
taught Italian encountered up north. Not
surprisingly, dealing with red tape was confusing and
frustrating. They learnt that they had to undergo a
medical examination to gain a medical certificate to
permit them to register with a doctor. They also had
to register themselves to the police and get their
Range Rover through state-approved checks to gain
its foreign car registration licence, thus allowing it to
be insured. Opening a bank account required not only
paper proof of their identity but local citizens to act as
witnesses to guarantee their character. Again,
neighbours were a great help to them in this bedding
down period of their lives, especially as their
elementary Italian was insufficient in negotiations
with officialdom. The effort was worth it as the right
documentation, allowed them to claim EU farming
subsidies, which reduced their financial burden and
helped conserve their savings.

The husband's main job was to get the house into a
state suitable for the modern era. This required
installing new electrical wiring and plumbing, the
reframing of windows and doors, the replacement of
broken flagstones and repairs to cracked roof tiles.
Walls required plastering and painting. The
stonework around the kitchen stove, come fireplace,
required repointing. On the insistence of Ruth, an
early priority was to cover the hole over the cesspit
and install a seat and cistern. Steve required time

away from the house to gather up tools, materials and get help to do the jobs properly. Every job done ate into their savings. The need to renovate meant there was no prospect of Steve finding paid work or creating artwork to raise income. Every time Steve left the house, he abandoned his wife in the Stone Age. He brought Jason back from Florence to help do some of the heavy work. This proved to be a waste of time as they spent most of their time lounging about or going into Naples. Ruth had naively taken up her role as a good wife in the hope of finding comfort within the confines of a relationship only to endure long periods of loneliness worse than she experienced when single. During her husband's absence, she had effectively swopped the loneliness of big city life for that of a foreign rural setting, a possible defenceless victim of any malevolent character looking for easy pickings. Steve's dog brought over from the home country offered no protection as it had similar roaming instincts as his master. Disappearing days on end and finally never to return, believed shot by a neighbour for harassing livestock. One Ear, the farmyard cat, became her confidante in these early days. The cat had lost part of its right ear one day in a fight with a wild animal. Its fur showed the scars of numerous fights and burns due to sleeping too close to the stove when hot splinters ignited its fur. There was no communication with the outside world or a straightforward highly visible way down the hill to the village. No telephone line or mobile phone masks within reach, and no quick exit leading to safety. Later, the neighbour down the hill would setup up a rope line through the trees with bells at each end to give her some way of raising an emergency alarm. In

the meantime, she remained invisible to the outside
world with all sound trapped by the surrounding
wood. The only motorised means of travel, the Range
Rover, routinely taken by Steve.

The quietude of the rustic setting gave Ruth plenty of
time for sober reflection. Thoughts dwelled on her
mind for longer than when life was artificially hectic.
She started to understand the true meaning of the
seasons. She came to enjoy the tranquillity of early
summer mornings when birds and animals were
accustomed to a few hours of bright light to go about
their business without fear of disruption or threat
from human activity. For the first time in her life, she
questioned herself and attempted to philosophise
about the meaning of life. Isolated in a cultivated
grove, she grew to like the countryside, a serenity only
interrupted by the sound of insects and sporadic calls
of disturbed birds as predators roamed around them.
Without light population, less cloud cover, being high
up and at a much lower altitude, her perspective of
the heavens changed. Sitting outside the farmhouse in
the warm evenings without good reading material,
she waited in silence as dusk gave way to night when
the sky put on its free show. In time, she was able to
discern many of its features. Her eyes turned skyward
with curiosity, awe and wonder. The cosmos was a
complex symphony, with all elements playing the
same song in counterpoint. She even knew when to
expect satellites and regular aircraft traffic to appear
across her own personal celestial spacescape. It was
no wonder that while her northern ancestors placed
the noon at the centre of their worship system, the
ancients here were astronomers who named star

clusters after their pantheon of Gods. Galileo not only discovered planets and their moons but saw the vast emptiness of space. She could feel the earth spinning eastwards as the panorama unfolded above her. She saw the expanse of Milky Way for the first time. The classical hero Hercules became her comforter during the summer months, whereas, in the winter months, Perseus watched over her. There was also the shotgun lying just behind the front door for additional protection.

Jason loved exploring Naples while Steve lusted after a dark slender working girl in a bar they acquainted on their visits to the subterranean city famed for shrines, secret passageways, burial chambers and crypts, catacombs and ancient ruins; a huge vigorous city teeming with life. In this city, people would have been obedient to the laws if there were justice, but old habits prevailed, corruption was ripe, and the impulse to do wrong or ignore rules was too strong. People had lost confidence in the many offices of law enforcement that existed here and had no faith in the political system. Crime and politics were good bedfellows. Away from the tourist spots, it was a world of small restaurants and bars with private rooms upstairs where working girls took their clients. Peregrinating the thronging streets required care as street quarrels, violent language, furious altercations in traffic, and boisterous behaviour could ignite at any time. The Neapolitan dressed beyond his or her means and more likely than not the male carried a knife for self-protection. Backstreet entrepreneurs went about their business, as above them balconies became forums for gossip, observation posts, and places to hang washing.

In narrow streets, streamers of laundry garland
across them. In daylight hours, market stalls
throughout the back streets were piled high with
goods. Fresh food, fruit and veg stalls selling local
produce, a region well known for its salami in all
shapes, chilli peppers, tomatoes and cheeses:
everything required to create the best pizzas known to
man. The waters off the coast were famous for its
anchovies. Steve loved the seafood on offer whereas
Jason stuck his nose up at spaghetti dishes containing
clams or rich anchovy sauce. As Steve preferred to
enjoy the food served in backstreet restaurants,
washed down with white wine or a glass of limoncello,
Jason opted to people watch in the main
thoroughfares drinking rich espresso served by
smartly uniformed waiters. Away from the secluded
villa in Tuscany, Jason saw at first hand the passion
that ordinary Italians had for their region and its
football team. The national game had many daily
sports papers dedicated to only reporting the latest
developments. Typical frictions between the friends
appeared as Jason's reluctance to emerge in the local
culture annoyed Steve, as it seemed to deliberately
miss the point about why he had opted for a change in
lifestyle. Whereas, Steve deliberately aped the local
mannerisms and quickly got into the habit of using
hand and eye signals to communicate colloquialisms.
In the end, Jason skedaddled back to Florence after
he had his fill of Naples as engaging life for real was
not his idea of foreign living. The further he travelled
from his homeland, the more stereotypically
condescending he became of other cultures. He
particularly found rural life in southern Italy a
strange alien world of incomprehensible gibbering

sounds when compared to the sophisticated northern Italian provinces.

As time went by the hard labour along with a Mediterranean diet did wonders for the couple's physique. They visibly got fitter, stronger and leaner over this period. Ruth's Rubenesque figure, dismissed in the eyes of the modern fashion-conscious world, gave her the strength required for an Apennine existence. Life eventually did get easier for Steve once he completed all the necessary work on the house, allowing a more leisurely pace to complete remaining work to smarten it up. This freed up time for him to drive into Naples looking for goods that would mark up well back in his native country, and to spend time in the village bar picking up hints on how to make life even easier. Ruth workload continued much the same, as there was no rest from chores in and around the house. Neighbours offered bits of furniture to help them out and soon the farmhouse looked the part with a genuine local interior containing few hi-tech additions. The news of a baby galvanised the locals. Most of the young had left the area years ago to find work up north or around Naples. Until their arrival, the average age was definitely over the official retirement age. The confinement of Ruth became public property with women coming out of the woodwork to offer help and advice. They helped her out with the formalities, as her Italian had not advanced much due to her isolation. She had to register with a paediatrician, as Italian doctors did not look after the health of mother and child. The paediatrician was responsible for the safeguarding of a child's welfare until the age of fourteen. Instructions for Ruth to rest when possible and to get Steve to do more about the house came to nothing as she lost patience waiting for Steve to do anything. Like the women around her, she used gossip to release any built-up tension. Sitting around kitchen tables, elders would sympathise with her, express their own childbearing experiences, and philosophically say that all men were lazy bastards. It was the women who endured a life of never-ending domestic drudgery: a daily routine of cleaning, polishing, cooking, laundering, ironing, seeing to the fireplace and stove as well as attending to the needs of the hens and pigs; chores, chores and more chores:

"All accomplished with our young holding on to the hems of our skirts."

"We were no better treated than the other livestock. When a hen stopped laying, it was chopped, bloodied, plucked and gutted while its younger replacement was introduced to the cock."

"Women were merely workhorses yoked by religion to serve man."

A retired priest made his way up the footpath from the village to pay Ruth a special visit to ascertain if she required help and more importantly to make her aware of her duties to safeguard the baby's soul. As a good shepherd, he wanted to ensure that the newborn had the protection of the Church and would learn about the gospels to give it comfort and some appreciation of morality. If personal qualities marked people out as selected by God to lead his people and to

protect them, it was testament to the old priest's own
faith to be confident that an eighty-year-old man
could comfortably walk up a steep stony path in the
heat of the middle of the day. Despite his years and
striking grey hair, he did look robust and strong-
minded. He still wore his old comfortable cassock with
a sturdy rope as a belt. His views reflected a strict
adherence to all the Catholic Canons with an
unbending belief on the right to rule of the Holy See
and that perdition awaited the unrepentant sinner;
strongly believing that God's work was unassailable
by human concepts and scientific thinking. It was a
case of not just acting holy but being holy. Although
retired, he continued to live in the diocese. On
occasions, he came out of retirement to fill in for the
current parish priest when called away due to
vacations, illness, religious seminars, or family
emergencies. Having time in old age to reflect seemed
to enhance his credentials, strengthening the right to
offer advice, regardless if requested or not. He
enquired about her health and if she was getting all
the support required. Ruth admitted that she was
concerned about raising a child in Italy with Steve.
The old priest pointed out that Italy was one of the
safest places on earth for children as they represented
the heart of the family. Most women desired babies
and having a husband was the right means to an end.
When you open the door to marriage, you have to
trust in God that the right man enters it. Marriage
was a sacred act. The gift of a baby was a blessing.
Domestic disputes were inevitable as man was
corporeal as well as spiritual so was not born perfect.
He required guidance from the Church on how to
subdue his passions and avoid temptations. Faith

was a great source of strength for helping to get through the trials and hardships encountered in life on earth. It gave life a meaning and purpose. With faith came responsibility. Prohibition of divorce and baptising children with the promise of raising them as Christians safeguarded the family. After Ruth admitted to being a lapsed Catholic, the old priest reiterated the importance of confession for her salvation. Confession allowed reconciliation with God. Redemption was also necessary from unintentional sin due to human weakness, shame and struggles with negative feelings. This aspect of confession was particularly important in marriages were things were done and said in the heat of the moment. The expressing of guilt to God's representative leads to guidance on improving behaviour in the eyes of God. The sacrifice of confession, praise and service allows cleansing and forgiveness leading to purification of the soul.

The rural setting did lend itself to the possibility of a divine plan. Whereas, the city with its distractions, modern cynicism and organised opposition by the many secular groups that existed did make it difficult for believers to not sometimes doubt their faith. In a remote countryside still farmed using traditional methods the stillness, openness and the acceptance of interdependency made it more plausible. When Ruth discussed the subject with Steve, he thought it was all mumbo-jumbo. If his years at a Jesuit school had taught him anything, it was that devotion to obtain salvation for a true believer was a vast undertaking. Morning prayers, spiritual exercises, and retreats to strengthen the bond with God and the Church, with strict obedience to the Ten Commandments. The list of do nots placed on man was endless. However, in the end, it was decided that their child would be brought up by following local traditions and that included the Church. The reason was one of practicality: they did not want the child discriminated against by appearing different. The gift of a crucifix and a portrait of Our Lady to adorn the front room cemented the covenant.

The local villagers were unassuming good-natured folk, easy going, straightforward, and very superstitious. In the village bar, the usual suspects played cards, acting to the manner born, ordering drinks and watching the world go by. Steve would join this company as wine and spirits became habitual drinks during the daytime. Playing cards was rewarding because the facial expressions of his drinking companions were full of contortions when thinking, making it easy to guess their hands. There was always a reason to celebrate due to the numerous religious and national holidays. They celebrated all the major Christian festivals and Republic day, there were national holidays for mother's day, St John the Baptist, the birthday of the Church at Pentecost, Our Lady of Madonna and many more. In the summer months, he drank in the surrounding villages, as they all had their own saint's day. Saints were available to and responsive to the prayers of the living as they were intermediaries between the Divinity and humankind. They had a voice to God enabling help for the sick and the creation of miraculous outcomes for worshippers. Men and women, young and old knelled in prayer before the shrine of the saint as the priest conducted mass, usually reciting the litany of All

Saints. Their village's saint was the archangel
Michael the guardian of the community from evil and
the slayer of the wicked. The villages tried to outdo
each other in zeal to get the best good fortune, decking
the streets with homemade bunting and strewing the
road with rose petals. For many, these festivals gave
an excuse for getting drunk and avoiding any work.
The women did all the preparation and the men from
all the area turned up to eat and drink until forced
back home by irate wives or overbearing mothers.

The paediatrician proved her worth by fixing Ruth up
with a bed in a maternity ward several days in
advance of the birth of her child, a girl named
Nanette. The arrival of Nanette was a celebrated
event for the village. Steve and Ruth sat at the table
of honour as gifts rained down on the beautiful little
baby. It was the baby's own personal *La Befana*. The
arrival of Nanette came at a cost. Ruth was not only
afflicted with more work but symptoms of depression
as well. It was the turning point in their relationship
as it dawned on Ruth that if she continued to let Steve
live the life of Reilly, she would become old and
haggard before her time. It was obvious that the baby
had made no impact on Steve's behaviour, as he
showed no signs of settling down or seeing the
farmhouse as his home. She became aware of mood
swings causing sadness, anxiety, and irritability. She
spent most of the day feeling tired and felt she had
made a mistake in having a child, which only
compounded the feeling of guilt for being selfish when
all her attention should be devoted to the baby. Steve
was unaffected by the newborn but suffered from
Ruth's irrational emotional outbursts and lack of

desire for sex. He also thought it was odd that a woman professing to be too tired for sex could be obsessed with cleaning the house. Unwanted, Steve decided to head out more often to Naples, hoping to seek out that dark slender girl or someone just as available. With great reluctance, Ruth decided to tell the paediatrician about her feelings and thoughts, and that she could not carry on like this. She had worried over the fear of not being able to clearly express her concerns in Italian. However, the paediatrician was extremely sympathetic and gave her a chit to take to the local hospital to allow her to get a full medical and treatment if required. They prescribed anti-depressants that subdued her rather than cured her. In the end, she remembered the advice of the old priest, bought an appropriate headscarf and went to confession the next time God's representative visited the village's chapel.

The population of the village was too small to maintain a fulltime priest so a district pastor priest looked after a commune of similar sized villages travelling between these villages to minister the flock. Each village maintained their chapel and prepared it for the arrival of the touring pastor and his acolytes. On each visit, the altar would be set up and then stripped away after the service. Ruth took her place in the chapel with those waiting to confess, wondering if she would be doing the right thing. When her turn arrived, the confessor did not hurry her, allowing her to express her emotions, fears and guilt. This act in itself made her feel better. She admitted feeling imprisoned by the Catholic laws on wedlock and admitted wishing to not have been impregnated with her husband's seed. It was reconfirmed to her that marriage was a sacrament demanded by God and she must atone for her selfish thoughts through devoted prayer. When she asked for forgiveness, the father gave absolution, instructing her to put faith in God's plan for her and to look after the child. Self-harm, whether it was physical or mental, was a mortal sin. She should resist it by thinking of the devotion of the Blessed Virgin Mary to baby Jesus. She was sent from the confessional to go and pray in the calm holy place of the chapel to become a better person.

Although not all the postnatal depression symptoms immediately went away, Ruth did feel better and build up resistance against pampering in self-pity. The old women naturally sided with Ruth when they saw how tired and overworked she looked whereas the lazy good for nothing Steve spent too much time in the village bar. The casting of the evil eye upon him happened on many occasions as he passed these old women but it did not cause any harm. Steve never broke a leg or went blind, or even sought help to get the evil lifted. Rumours spread that Priapus must be protecting him. Ruth did learn to be more forthright in expressing her frustration constructively. Good mothers tend to find the strength necessary to stand up and fight for the benefit of her child and Ruth was no different. The days when she tolerated his spending and impromptu disappearances were ending.

Nanette was baptised on mother's day. A day celebrated in the village with a procession from the chapel to the shrine of the Holy Mother and the

Blessed Child situated on a high outcrop overlooking
the village on the other side of the valley from their
farmhouse. It was a day when relatives and grownup
offspring returned to the area bringing their own
children with them. The place would be noisy again
with young voices. Makeshift stalls with embroidered
sheets placed on the streets, displayed statuettes of
the crucifixion and of the Madonna with baby Jesus,
alongside portraits of the pope, past and present.

The peeling of the chapel bell signalled the start of the
procession to the shrine. Everyone positioned
themselves to watch the passing of it. The doors of the
little chapel swung open to reveal patches of
candlelight escaping from the darkness. First, the
crucifer appeared, a novice in his cassock, flanked by
two choirboys in their white robes waving incense.
Behind them the canopy held by other choirboys to
protect the chapel's statue of Saint Anne with a young
Mary. The priest clothed in his liturgical vestments
marched behind with the remaining choirboys who
held candlesticks or prayer books. To the rear came
the grandchildren of the local families trooping behind
their mother's day banner depicting the Venerated
Mary and the baby Jesus, children in their Sunday
best trying to pick out family members in the crowd.
In their hands were votive offerings of flowers and
fruit. Finally, old women seeming to be doing
penitents followed the procession as it slowly made its
way out of the village. This last group of pilgrims
murmured Hail Marys as rosaries turned one bead at
a time in their hands. Ruth recognised all the women
and wondered what they had confessed at their age to
cause such contrition. Police cleared the main road

that cut across the route to the stony path up to the
outcrop. All the way out of the village children too
young to partake in the procession, with the help of
their mothers, scattered handful of rose petals in front
of the procession. As the procession disappeared into
the wood, the stalls were cleared and laid with food
and drink to celebrate the return of the pilgrims. On
such occasions, even the old priest accepted a free
drink from the village bar.

Soon after the baptism, Steve fell out of love with this
existence. It seemed a good idea but in practice, rural
life was turning into a nightmare as the realities of
genuine subsistence living kicked in when financial
restrictions reduced his opportunities for adventure. A
languor settled in his mind as Ruth took on most of
the farmhouse duties. He was throwing away the best
years of his life by remaining here. The demands on
him to become responsible and accountable now that
he was a father became intolerable. The child seemed
to him to have given Ruth a strength that chastised
his influence over her. Initially, this newly found
strength was just a thorn in his side but as time went
by living on pin money from a frugal wife became a
grudge that festered into open strife. Month after
month, his world got smaller until he spent most of
his time in the village bar. It became predictable and
boring. No one in the village had money to burn and
made their drink last. He felt he was going mad,
because of the boredom and having no one to exploit.
He became restless and anxious from feeling trapped
in a somewhat claustrophobic, static and unengaging
environment that could not any longer continue to
hold interest, meaning, or value to him. This

predicament resulted in outbursts of agitation caused by frustration of not being able to continue with his carefree existence. He had lost interest in the peasant community and with Ruth. He stopped listening to her and deliberately became untidy about the house. He found the sex boring. At home, he would sit in his corner, teasing the cat or Nanette while drinking homemade grappa. All the plans to give the farmhouse a face-lift remained just plans. He was not prepared to continue the life he carved out; the bare necessities of life were not for him, he needed to befriend fun seekers. He also dreaded the idea that he would descend into the same state he found Martin the last time he saw him. Meanwhile, Ruth's resolution in ensuring that any spare money went on Nanette was creating an effective emotional barrier between Steve and her. It gave her a purpose and the will to endure anything thrown at her.

Steve became antagonistic and deliberately made himself unbearable by vexing Ruth with sudden inconvenient change of plans and bringing up issues meant to annoy her. His drinking became excessive and a danger to everyone, even himself. He would drive home or stumble up the path from the village when drunk. When entering the house, he would always nearly smash a pane of glass with his shoulder as he lurched at the door. Ruth would try to laugh it off and manhandle him up to the bedroom to get him to sleep off the drunkenness. She did her best to portray the patience of a saint. Sometimes, his reluctance to go to sleep was too strong as he pushed past her to sit in his favourite corner. He could be a savage beast when drunk, arguing for argument sake.

Ruth would constantly have to remember her confessional vows to maintain peace for the sake of the child and play down the deliberate attempts to start a fight. On some occasions, he would knock her down and trample on her when she attempted to get him to go to their bedroom to sleep off the drink. When sober, he would not acknowledge any misdemeanours. On a positive note, Nanette's young age along with Ruth's pacifism protected the child from any long-term adverse effects.

Throughout this period, Steve could spoil the child with attention as she provided a diversion from his boredom. He was capable of switching from being a caring father to a rough forceful lover when the opportunity presented itself. On one such occasion, he took Nanette to bed holding One Ear in one arm and the child in the other. With Nanette tucked up in bed stroking the cat, he recited his own tale of the cat and the magpie to help her get to sleep:

"Once upon a time, a cat stalked a magpie, hoping to one day catch it and torment it. However, the magpie would always escape the clutches of the cat, fly away and perch on a nearby tree. The cat would inevitably attempt to climb up the upward pointing branches of this tree to get at the magpie. Each day it managed to climb a little higher and each day the magpie skipped up a few more branches. To human ears, it seemed that the meowing and the chuckling that took place during their game was just incoherent noise. In fact, they were having a conversation as the upward movement of both creatures maintained the same distance between them. The magpie was always asking

the cat why it could not understand that it was superior to it, and the cat was wasting its time trying to catch it. The cat should just give up and move on in life. The cat was having none of it as it insisted that with a little more effort it would reach the magpie and have its fun. This type of conversation went on and on for days until one day, the magpie could not skip up any further as the cat by sheer willpower and all its agility had climbed up the thinnest of branches to be within touching distance of the magpie. I have you at last said the cat as it made its final push upwards. The cunning magpie sarcastically chuckled then flew in the air just above the tree. The bending branch without the additional weight of the bird quickly straightened up causing the cat to catapult off the tree. It rolled in the air and landed awkwardly on a nearby patch of grass. The magpie flew down next to the suffering cat and said that it admired its tenacity but it should really find another creature to try to torment, one that was inferior to it so negating the chance of self-harming events it had just experienced. The cat reluctantly agreed saying it would spend its time from now on catching squirrels. The magpie queried its new choice, as the squirrel was a relative of the rat and so was probably a species still too clever and quick for it. The magpie suggested man would be a more appropriate creature to tease and torment. The cat has ever since that day specialized on manipulating and tormenting man. It tamed him, got him to accept that his role was to feed it and to keep his house warm for it. So, when you saw a cat meowing up at the magpie on its high perch it was just a conversation about how the cat was progressing with the taming of man, with the magpie was forever reminding the cat to keep its *instructions simple as possible as man was not capable of deep underst*anding."

Nanette loved his story and continually asked for it. Afterwards, Steve went straight downstairs, seized Ruth with a tight grip and fondled her. She was defenceless. Greedy for pleasure, he aroused himself by talking dirty to her, and then deliberately exposed himself as he allowed her to move them both into the kitchen to be out of earshot of Nanette. She had feared being beaten if she did not allow him satisfaction. He forced her to lean over the table complaining about the amount of underclothes she had on. The objects on the tables were sent clattering, smashing and thudding onto the stone floor depending on whether they were metals, ceramics or vegetables. Her neck cracked under his strong arm as her eyes gazed straight ahead at the sink and the sky beyond the window above it. Her clothes pulled down, he touched her up and pinched her backside supposedly to stimulate her. Her pleas and utterances did not spare her; they only encouraged her husband's excitement. Virtue had to succumb to brutal force. When it came to sexual intercourse, he was not potent for long and resorted to using an unripe courgette to finish her off. It was an intended act of humiliation. His manhood was the only weapon left to him to extract punishment. A punishment for upsetting the natural state of things by withdrawing funds he required to have a good life. Afterwards, he poured himself a drink, completely ignoring the hate expressed by Ruth's facial expression and body language.

Her misgivings about their relationship severely
conflicted with the desire to follow Church guidance
on marriage, and to keep the family together for the
child's sake. Furthermore, she was pregnant again.
Periods of calm did sometimes replace the flip-flop
character changes that manifested as tenderness
followed by sadistic acts. They had even some good
times especially concerning the adventures of a
growing and inquisitive Nanette. Nonetheless, the
relationship was tainted and resentment always
simmered away in the background. In the calmer
periods, Steve was on his best behaviour, minding his
manners, all the time formulating a plan to allow him
to return to a more carefree existence. Various
schemes entered his head on how to end this part of
his life. Some instantly dismissed as too radical. Like
orchestrating an apparently accidental death, then
claiming insurance had financial advantages but he
was not completely heartless to abandon Nanette
alone in a foreign land. Taking her with him would
have defeated the object. A mother and child had a
better chance of survival. In the meantime, he
withdrew small steady amounts of money from the
family savings account, enough to build up a nest egg
without drawing too much suspicion.

A sudden jerk on the earth's surface fifty kilometres
away signalled an earthquake. Early reports indicated
many deaths at the epicentre. Nearer to home, the
farmhouse juddered, tiles fell off the roof, ceilings and
walls cracked, utensils broke as they fell on the floor,
and outside the livestock scattered about in confusion
after an enclosure wall gave way. In the village, some
fires broke out to cause damage to property, no one

died. The only major incident was a landslide that cut off the area from the rest of the world for a few days. For Steve, it was the final straw that gave impetus to move on, as staying would mean months of work to repair the house, which would exhaust the last of the savings to pay for it.

Fissures caused by domestic frictions now became incurable open sores. He recommenced his trips into Naples supposedly looking for merchandise to sell on to raise money for repairs. Earlier visits to prostitutes meant that low-level criminal elements knew him and he knew them. These low-level criminal elements themselves had contacts with members within the Camorra. Steve decided to approach them to see if they could help him with his predicament. After some hesitancy and confirmation of his authenticity by checking with their police contacts to make sure he was not a plant, they agreed to offer their services. Whether it was a vendetta, a kidnapping or murder they could help. The level of violence used was negotiable but it affected the price. A single bullet solution to his problem would only require a shooter while any requirement for torture would entail at least two men, resulting in higher overheads. The price depended on how far up the command chain approval had to be sought to permit the final go ahead. Steve made sure that they understood that he only wanted to disappear, nothing else. It was only a case of disentanglement from an undesired situation. No liquidation was necessary. They reassured him that this was a straightforward transaction not requiring high-level approval from leaders in the top clans within the organisation. People disappeared all the time in Italy to avoid taxes or criminal convictions. They could sort out a new identity for him in a couple of weeks. All he had to do was pay half the amount up front and the other half when he received his new papers. Because he did not look like a southerner, they decided to make his new identity that of a northerner, born near the border. Steve used the damage caused by the earthquake to get a secured loan from the bank to supposedly do repairs. As this required Ruth's approval as well, he obtained it by forging her signature. The sum obtained effectively wiped out all the remaining family savings held in accounts solely managed by Ruth.

On the day of this departure, he got up early, loaded the Range Rover with his essentials, drove to the nearest petrol station, filled the tank and vanished. It was a beautiful day, a day when a marriage of six years ended. He was a free man again with his thirst for life renewed; just being on the road again made him feel better. The swiftness of his exit contrasted remarkably with the months spent creating acrimonious confrontations to destroy all emotional attachment Ruth had ever developed for him. Although Ruth half expected him to walk out on them, prepared or unprepared, it still came as a shock when she finally realised what had happened. It actually took Ruth several days to come to this conclusion as at first, she assumed he was off on another adventure; days that subsequently revealed a credit card trail all the way up Italy before the bank annulled the card. He left her in despair as the money had run out and she was stranded without transport. Fortunately, community spirit and sentiment saved the day.

Neighbours and the Church rallied round her, offered help and advice that in due course put her back on her feet. Ruth's need to survive and carry on safeguarding the unborn child and the young Nanette prevented her from collapsing into an emotional wreck. She developed a hardness that surprised her. Nothing from now on would distract or stop her from bringing up the children in a safe and loving environment. The family came first. She found when tested, that she possessed courage. She got a bit of luck when the district obtained EU grants to modernise its infrastructure and habitats. Money poured in to improve the roads to reduce travel times, to improve sanitation and to connect remote farmhouses like hers to the national electricity grid and water supplies. All this improvement drastically increased the value of the property as city professionals could now commute to work in Naples.

The single parent family eventually moved to a nearby town where Ruth found work and Nanette attended school. The second child was a boy, called Giuseppe, named after the old priest, and he would grow up to look like his father, which vexed his devoted mother, as it seemed like another cruel punishment. However, the absence of a bad example of a father figure engendered beneficial effects on everyone. Ruth no longer felt stifled and developed a more outgoing personality. Nanette was destined to turn into a fiery stubborn pale looking red-haired Italian that knew what she wanted. Maybe, the bedtime tale of the cat taming man stayed with her, as she would make sure that no man ever got the better of her. More likely, it was the example of a strong female role model in the shape of her mother that strengthened her character. Growing up in a non-threatening environment meant the boy developed a healthy good-natured disposition. With mother and sister looking after him, he was not short of love as a child. A strong intimate familial bond held all them together. None of the children developed any interest in the whereabouts or status of their father. In their early years, they were more upset and disturbed by the natural death of the old One Ear than their father's disappearance. As for Steve, he vowed that in the future there be no mundane domestic setting, no wife or children with all the pressures that came with them or getting trapped in a place with no easy opportunities to get money, nothing to come between him and his happiness. To preserve his youthful spirit, he required a bachelor's life that embraced risk-taking activities.

The prevailing opinions in the community were they always knew that Steve was no good, a vassal of Satan, and that the labours of Ruth would be recompensed in her next life. The lasting memory of this human tragedy was that folklore would record how the archangel Michael once again drove evil out of the village.

COUNCIL DUTIES

When local government duties called, Steve prepared
himself for circular bureaucratic discussions about
trivia or rubber-stamping petitions from local
businesses or private landlords. At council meetings,
there were not sufficient numbers of elected members
to allow anyone to hide at the back of the chambers.
No possibility of watching something more interesting
on a laptop or smartphone until the time came to vote
or agree to carry any discussion on to the next
meeting. Everyone sat around a table while the chair
of the meeting went through the formal procedures
loved by all bureaucrats. A town clerk took the
minutes so it was a case of sitting up straight and
listening to the usual suspects make their cases for or
against the proposals under discussion. All he had to
do was pay attention for keywords like environment
or pollution to alert him. Enterprise and other public
sponsored quango meetings followed the same pattern
except for the personal assistant of the board's chair
took all the notes. Usually these meetings lasted
about two hours, following a familiar fixed format:
coffee on arrival, a recording in the minutes of those
present, a review of the previous minutes, a report on
possible developments, and an open question session,

recording of minutes then a late lunch or afternoon tea and finally claiming of expenses.

Nothing useful ever happened at the quangos or council sub-committee meetings that Steve attended, which actually explained the nominations for Steve to be on them in the first place. All new councillors ended up on committees that experienced councillors avoided. These old foxes preferred to monopolise committees that wheeled influence and had a high profile with the local press so consequently the public. In short, any real or significant development would occur with or without the consent of any committee or quasi-board on which Steve was a member. Other committees made the big decisions. His job was to back these decisions, rubberstamp them. Bureaucracy existed for its own benefit and rewarded Steve with expenses for his attendance. The fact that close examination of the minutes of any meeting he ever attended showed no sufficient contribution attributed to his name was neither here or there. If any real commercial opportunity for the town arose then obstacles would quickly be swept aside with regional aid grants found. The commercial district in town was stagnant and cried out for a fresh impetuous so anything legal or environmentally neutral would pass all the planning permission stages if a big national player ever wanted to set up a base in town. The creation of new jobs was paramount. Therefore, Steve could never be accused of holding back progress and was only fulfilling a role that any other new councillor would do. On the other hand, personal opportunities sometimes opened up for him.

In particular, he was presently surprised with the unexpected outcome from attending a bi-annual local enterprise board meeting. The attract business and financial opportunities at any cost brigade within the council did not have a majority and so required consensus to get controversial proposals pass early committee stages through to a full council vote. Steve's amenability drew this element's attention. It meant that an unbelievable auspicious opportunity was about to be presented to him, which would change the town forever as well as thrust him into the stratosphere as far as personal gain was concerned. A consortium of property developers on behalf of eminent clients had been perusing their part of the south coast, as it was within easy reach of up town, looking for a location to turn into a private resort. The benign climate, natural lay of the land and its closeness to the Downs and chalk cliffs made the town an ideal place for consideration.

As Steve was leaving the meeting, a fellow councillor pulled him into a corner to invite him for a quick drink at a nearby hotel. Ever sociable he accepted the invitation whereupon a polished personal relations consultant introduced himself. This led to a good hour spent listening to this harbinger of potential investment opportunities, explaining the bleak future of any seaside town if it did not welcome changes that met the needs of the wealthy. All the time sounding Steve out to see if he was a man of strong principle or a chap who would happily grasp the opportunity for personal gain. The consultant had no need to worry and a second meeting was arranged where more details from the consortium would explain what

precise opportunities there was to be had for an
ambitious town and its forward-thinking councillors.

This meeting took place over a private lunch at a
health spa out of town. The consortium's marketing
team explained to the assembled responsive
councillors that their backers instructed them to find
a town that would be amenable to the building of a
state of the art marina for clients that required
moorings large enough to berth large luxury cruisers.
Hayes-by-the-Sea was a prime candidate for the
development because it allowed quick passage to the
continent, had the right terrain and was, of course,
within easy reach by helicopter or fast roads from up
town. The money involved in this project was huge
and would put the town on the map again. Money
attracts money so there would be no end of
opportunities for everyone. In short, they wanted the
councillors to help them purchase the old harbour,
warehouses and adjacent lands to redevelop the
seafront. The highest authorities in the land had
already given their clients the unofficial go-ahead to
pursue this adventure. They now required local help
to overcome any obstacles that could slow down or
frustrate their attempts to bring prosperity to their
region. If they welcomed this broad outline of future
development then further details with explanations
would be forthcoming but only after they signed
confidentiality contracts with the consortium.

Without hesitation, Steve merrily signed the non-
disclosure document then went home to report to Mi-
Cha the opportunity of making a killing by buying
more property before news of this new development

became public knowledge. With financial backing from Korea, they would go on to purchase several additional flats under Mi-Cha's family name. The local estate agents noticed a little housing boom as other knowledgeable councillors passed on the same news to friends and relatives. Fortunately, for the councillors and the upkeep of integrity, no one else noticed it and so it was full steam ahead as far as supporting the construction of a state of the art marina.

An invite to an up town two-day presentation at a prestigious location duly arrived, a billion-pound structure by the river designed by internationally renowned architects for a private company owned by an alliance of Arab sultans. The two-day event would be the most polished and professional event Steve had ever encountered. Steve felt shabby in his best suit and vowed thereafter to up his dress sense. The marketing company organising the event had many illustrious customers and knew how to impress their targeted audience. The list of non-executive directors displayed behind their reception desk was a who's who of ex-cabinet ministers and city financial gurus. All men but more pertinently public school educated. The marketing company knew how to push the boundary of honest business practices to just a hairs-breadth within the law, or when duty called left no proof of any committed crime. All their perfectly groomed staff wore sharp expensive business suits and gave the impression of being first class honour students from Oxbridge. Their voices were smooth, articulate and very polite. They were obviously people of considerable intelligence, representing the best this country had to offer to the world; not scientists, engineers or welfare specialists, something more important than the doers, they were the fixers, the facilitators and the personal relation experts. They knew the right people to connect together to maximise gains. Their suits went with the sharp practices employed to get what their customers demanded.

Waiters served the finest coffee and petite continental sweet pasties as they gathered in a private suite with outstanding views of the river and historic buildings along it. A celebrated ex-international footballer welcomed them to the event and hoped that they would find it instructive as he passed out brochures illustrating the proposed development. The brochures were not to leave the premises, as the details within them were commercially sensitive. The financial backing, the proposal itself and impact on the community still had to be finalised. The ex-footballer's presence indicated immediately that this was a well-funded project with potentially big returns for the backers. He was a marketing company's dream as the public and press both adored him. His face could sell anything from perfume to unit trusts. Although he never had anything interesting to say and could come across stiff or even a bit thick, the media fell over themselves to photograph him. Because the media accepted his vacuous image, they never questioned his judgement. At the same time, he could be trusted to just front a product while others sold its merits. Behind that face, public relations experts had built up a successful commercial enterprise. His true personal, social and political views were unknown to anyone but trusted confidants. Maybe, the image of him continually globetrotting to earn money he could never hope to spend was only a media creation and in reality, he spent many a night at home relaxing reading a good book. If he was always dedicating his life only in the pursuit of wealth then there may have been a shrewd plan behind it. Perhaps, his accrued vast wealth would ultimately finance a private army to overthrow parliament to allow him to declare himself dictator and true friend of the people. No doubt, the media to a man would unhesitatingly support this coup.

There would only be four presentations with durations of ninety minutes, which suggested that a one-day event would have sufficed. However, the main purpose of the event was to impress the guests and to determine the motivations of all the councillors to tailor individual remuneration packages to engender complete loyalty to the project. Basic groundwork by private investigators had produced dossiers for the psychoanalysts within the marketing team to ponder, but face-to-face contact would allow them to pinpoint precise weaknesses and cravings to which to deploy specific hooks to pull them in. Steve to their delight was an uncomplicated fellow, who always only considered the present without any due concern for the future. He was also new to this game, so did not know his worth to the consortium. Good meals, plenty of backslapping, a top class overnight stay, acuminating in the gift of an otherwise out of his league expensive ex-miss world contestant call girl did him fine. The last inducement obtained through an intermediary at an evening celebrity bash they attended, a bash that gave out goody bags, in his case an augmented goody bag worth tens of thousands of pounds.

The two-day event would also be useful to ascertain concerns any councillor had on how they would sell the package of proposals to members or supporters of their own political group. For this task, a team of consultants and script writers assigned to each of them stood ready to produce a sales pitch emphasising the merits from a free trade, social democrat or environmental standpoint: profitability, creation of jobs, architecture for a climate affected world, they could spin the proposal anyway.

The first session disclosed information about the finances behind the proposal. A bank bailed out after the global financial collapse by an Arab prince acting as a private citizen rather than the head of a foreign state, would make funds available to a consortium of billionaires, each of them having promised to underwrite the costs by guaranteeing two hundred million if losses occurred. Twenty billionaires had signed up to the project, giving promised guarantees of four billion. Most of the billionaires came from the Arabian Gulf with a few Russians, Asians and South Americans making up the numbers. Apart from money, they all had one other thing in common, a love for sailing. The depth of silence that engulfed the room contrasted with the wideness of the gaping mouths of every one of the assembled councillors. If the councillors were screaming then the pitch was well above the scales for even a dog to hear. Needless to say, the wide smiles on the faces of the marketing team reflected their pleasure at the reaction of the councillors.

Lunch lasted well over two hours. The venue was just a few blocks away. The dining room was a Georgian banqueting hall with an array of French windows that opened out into an enclosed manicured garden. It was more like a rebellious office Christmas party than a formal meal between potential antagonists, where one group represented cut-throat venture capitalism and the other the guardians of public welfare. Wine and spirits flowed with the charm that oozed from friendly hosts as they conversed in first name terms with comfortably relaxed guests. Steve had fun deliberately recalling the least amusing anecdotes he knew just to see the false laughter lines spontaneously appear on the face of the host dedicated to his table. Wondering all the time whether these people were great actors or had they totally morphed into the role work had given them so that they could not now distinguish between genuine and false behaviour. Creating a caricature that incarcerated them inside the world of work. The mask of his host never cracked as he held his professionalism, not revealing any glimpse of human feeling.

The afternoon session was a presentation of a promotion video outlining the intentions the consortium had for their town. The opening image projected onto the screen was a still aerial shot of the beach and the old harbour. Gradually the original image faded away to be overlaid with what could only be described as a computer-generated futuristic vision of a clean bright tomorrow. The components of this vision became clearer to the audience as the plane of view swept down and moved between the computer-generated structures. The voice of a well-known actor narrated the vision of tomorrow explaining how architects of today harnessed the latest technology to produce the world of tomorrow. The complex was designed by a team of Dutch architects whose reputation was built on the production of iconic structures in the near and Far East. The early modernists used rectilinear classical Euclidean geometry to design functional structures. Horizontal and the vertical lines constituted the shape and décor of everything from the walls, roof planes, and balconies, which either slide passed or intersected each other. Now architects deconstructed this fixed vision, deliberately creating disorder with random forms of high complexity using non-Euclidean geometry. Thanks to advanced computing techniques, complex mathematical engineering and inversion modelling, they could produce designs allowing the banishment of sharp aggressive boundaries resulting in designs with minimal surfaces, structures spiralling to the stars, with the use of curvatures, hyperboloids, lattices, quatrefoils, and parabolic arches. Optimum use of space achieved by combining hexagon and pentagon cellular elements. Strengthened glass and modern materials used to produce bold, bright and colourful structures that reflect, diffuse or refract light. Hyperbolic geometry offered economy in the design of tall structures such as towers where the hyperboloid geometry's structural strength supported an object high off the ground. A tower was the potent symbol of man and the centre point of any modern city scaping. The effort expended to design and built these structures reflected the ambition and will of a successful society.

Buildings had a lifespan that lasted over one hundred years throughout which they consumed energy and produced emissions. The lifespan of a building, therefore, merited considerable investment in the design phase to reduce these signatures, particularly as preservation was part of the armoury to obtain sustainability. However, buildings also reflected the ambition of a society and shaped the landscape around it. Iconic structures pushed back the boundaries in the use of materials and design. Consequently, present designers owed it to future generations to expand knowledge to build better new structures. The primary function of a building was to provide shelter, after this first objective, they became places of pleasure. The richer you were the more pleasure you wanted. We lived in an age when there were copious numbers of rich looking for fitting places to spend their time. People liked to be with others like themselves. The rich were no different. Rich people only wanted to associate with other rich people so this development would offer that opportunity. It would have every facility required to those who could afford a fabulous long weekend or short holiday break. It would be a resort offering a piazza fill of first-class shopping and restaurants; with aquariums, a health centre with spas, swimming pools, saunas and massage parlours, a sports centre, a golf range and stables to gallop horses on the Downs; and, of course, the marina would attract luxury cruisers and major yachting events.

The vision did look stunning. There was a new private

road on the outskirts of the east side of the town connecting the resort directly to the motorway one mile north of the town. When entering the resort from this road you would see the sports centre, golf range, stables and polo pitches on your left. On your right was a heliport with ample parking for helicopters, then a car park and a new massive breakwater. The road led behind the first long condominium that ran the length of one side of the marina to a dropping off point next to a welcoming water feature designed as a tribute to Jane Austen and her short stay in the town. An exquisite use of small shards of hollow clear glass with uplighting to signify a blossomed flower garden with fountains and platinum statues of young frolicking Georgian ladies, dressed in bonnets and long flowing flimsy revealing gowns, holding watering cans or wicker baskets in their hands. The changing colour of the uplighting produced the impression of movement through different types of flowers as a mist of fine spray from the shards of glass engulfed the whole scene. The road then continued past the back of another condominium, ending at the base of the second new breakwater. The condominiums were identical with one hundred luxury flats over five storeys raised above ground level with parking underneath them. Each flat had a wide balcony with a view of the marina. A projected view from a balcony showed the marina protected by the long curving ten-metre high breakwaters that ran out of the shore at each end of the complex to within sixty metres touching distance. In the centre of this artificial bay was a man-made island supporting the linchpin of the design. From the fountain, a wide esplanade through the condominiums led to a fifty-metre long causeway connecting the island to the shore. A broad promenade ran in front of the condominiums, around the island and the inner side of the breakwaters, which was tiered with the inner side four-metres lower than the higher outer protection, steps every one hundred metres allowed access to the top of the outer walls. The promenades were wide enough to cope with cyclists and electric buggies to transport goods and people. Along the condominiums and sea walls café, bars with outside parasol covered sitting gave the place a continental feel. The island and promenades along the seafront and the inner side of the breakwaters had sufficient moorings for at least twenty super-size cruisers and two hundred smaller crafts.

The centrepiece was a large multi-purpose tower that sat on the island, a twenty-four-storey four-side pyramid structure with a flat roof to accommodate a heliport. The design of the structure incorporated panelling that emitted and reflected light in a variable and distinctive way. The appearance of the building would change to reflect the different seasons. It was a modern-day Pharos that made its presence known to the world. The ground floor was open to the elements to allow easy access to mingle around aquariums, exhibition areas, stalls and bars. The shopping piazza was on the first floor. Floors two to four were restaurant and leisure areas. An exclusive upmarket hotel with a casino took up the fifth through to the fourteenth floor. Residential suits were between floors fifteen and twenty-two. The remaining top floors housed reception and observation areas.

Dredging within the sea walls to a suitable depth would allow luxury cruisers to berth safely. A submersible barrier at the entrance to the marina protected the complex during significant sea surges. Concrete slabs mixed with rushed quartz paved the promenades to create a long lasting sparkling grey sheen. Rainwater gathered on roofs and stored in tanks would reduce the demand for non-potable water so safeguarding supplies to the town. Solar panels, geothermal heat pumps and boilers powered by wood pellets augmented electricity and hot water requirements. Captured heat and light would maintain an ambient eighty Fahrenheit temperature within the complex. Cannabis or rather, hemp mixed with lime would provide building insulation. In hot weather, solar-controlled louvres on the glass frontages stopped the buildings from over-heating. The presentation ended with applause from the appreciative audience.

The evening's entertainment lived up to expectations and after a cocaine-fuelled night of passion, Steve woke up alone to persistent knocks on the hotel room door; a massive hangover and the shakes reminded him of his exertions. The only thing that immediately came to mind was that his over forty-year-old body had somehow held out and he was still alive. The evening had started off sedately enough as all the delegates met in the hotel lounge around seven to have an appetizer, where each one of them was given a debit card to use at their own discretion. Then out of the attractions presented to them, Steve opted for a gala with the stars. Once conveyed to the venue and after he was introduced to his escort for the evening, he quickly lost contact with the other delegates and his chaperone from the consultancy. The escort was the aforementioned ex-miss world contestant, who represented an island off the mainland of Asia. The pair wandered around the gala for only an hour until Steve became completely bored with it all. The incessant self-congratulatory tone of the event spoilt the taste of the fine liquors being freely offered by busy agile waiters.

Steve decided the debit card in his pocket should be put to use to ensure that he had a night to remember. He had the means to be king for the day so he planned to make himself the centre of attention. Flagging down taxis, he reacquainted himself with familiar artistic haunts where he freely bought drinks for any old drinking companions encountered. He showed off his pedigree tart to them: a tart that only wore a tight short sparkling dress not designed for quick movement in and out of taxis or standing in cold draft ridden bars while being gawked at by passers-by and pub regulars used to inferior eye candy. She was passed off as his latest muse. He even tried to do his bit for the country by probing the tart for names of any illustrious clients to pass on to the secret service. The final destination was a celebrity jazz club where they engaged in a bit of fondling in a dark corner. They then went back to the hotel room with cocaine purchased at one of the bars. Like a drunk on a Saturday night that cannot really distinguish between a late-night snack of gourmet food from stew made with dog pooh, Steve went through the motions of sexual play with only a hint of appreciation of the quality that was under him. Her skin may have been smoother and softer but nothing special stuck in his mind afterwards. If he ever dwelled with fondness on previous exploits then the dark-skinned whore in Naples would always come to the fore as his best lay. In the early morning, his companion expertly tiptoed out of the hotel room, shutting the door without disturbing him.

The representative sent to round up the councillors for day two of the presentation had come prepared. He dished out uppers to get those in need of help in getting back on their feet, explaining the same stimulants kept world leaders on their feet during all night crises talks. The downside being that once the effects wore off they would sleep for twenty-four hours. The ex-footballer again welcomed them by handing out briefing notes on behalf of the consortium backed by foreign billionaires. The second day presentations centred on pep talks and strategies to adopt to sell the project to their constituents; slanting the debate to concentrate on the merits of the proposal to win support for it and downplaying any detrimental arguments.

The motivational guest speaker for the pep talk was a former UN peace envoy and political leader with private business interests in the United Arab Emirates. His PR agency had a consultancy office there. His agency advised the Emirates and neighbouring countries on how to improve their perception to the international media. Embassy officials routinely briefed him but were not always sure of what he was doing and exactly whom he was representing, as he was now a paid employee of Arab state-owned companies so may unintentionally not be representing our national interests. Some considered him a dangerous hawk: an unwanted presence in this strategic region.

He ardently addressed them about the role they must play in the coming months and years. He enthused about the opportunities on offer. It was a scary, uncertain and exciting time with no clear dividing line to tell apart the good and bad guys, a time full of opportunity for the brave. On the world stage, due to heritage and the likes of Churchill and Thatcher this country had gained respect and punched above its weight. Diplomatic and cultural links extended around the world. It was incredibly important to keep it that way. To tilt the balance of power in our favour required the courage to engage in the global market. It was important to take the lead when endearing ourselves to the super-rich. They were crucial allies. Everyone had to be global players adapting to the new world order if the country was to thrive; parochialism was the biggest threat to prosperity.

Humanity was entering a dangerous period. The right or wrong of actions done to safeguard progress was relative, no longer restricted by artificial constraints or niceties. No one had clean hands in world affairs so it was hypocritical to condemn the misdemeanours of our friends. History judged us, not morality. World population growth alongside rapid urbanisation of developing countries in Asia meant more countries competing to offer high-end knowledge-based commodities and business services at a time when demand for limited natural resources had increased.

Globalization was here to stay. There was no turning back. Internet shopping was the prime example for the reason why everyone had to engage with global capitalism. Customers here triggered a sale in America for goods made in China transported to this country by a shipping line owned by Middle East oligarchs with the bill processed in Switzerland, Ireland or Holland to avoid tax duties. Labyrinths existed everywhere. Nothing was black or white anymore.

There was an increased risk to the global markets due to the higher probability of cataclysmic disruption in the future because of human conflict, pandemics and environmental disasters. The Internet allowed terror groups to deliver their message of hate to every online user on the planet. Therefore, trade and good relations with all countries was of strategic importance and overrode everything else. We must do business with undemocratic states and potentates who do not believe in universal freedoms, human or workers' rights. As a free trade nation, we could not afford to give up a strong relationship with our allies. The battlefield was no longer social justice but embracing the global market by keeping the super-rich on our side. We had to tolerate the whims of the super-rich or they would go elsewhere. The Arabian royal families and their cohorts could easily provide material and financial support to rivals or even to religious extremists bent on terrorism.

Nowadays no one accurately remembered anything after a couple of days. Once emotions subsided, people moved on to more practical matters. Therefore, any uproar against unethical practices created by the news media putting their own interests before those of the country was only a temporary blip. We must facilitate business opportunities to keep people in work. Diplomacy was about the evasion of unfortunate unpleasant truths. At the end of the day, what was good for you was good for the country. The public expected its leaders to lead them. Always promote the positive and ignore the negatives. The masses demanded jobs and affordable commodities. Concerns about human rights did not put food on the table. It was their job to make hard decisions as most experts in their field only provided explanations for problems. They rarely came forward to demand vigorous action, as they did not want to live with the consequences. The session ended with the joyous announcement that when the proposed harbour development became public knowledge the charm offensive would begin in earnest. Interested parties in the Emirates would formally invite delegates as honoured guests to their region to see at first hand the achievement of sustainable living in architecturally inspirational environments.

An in-house served lunch allowed discrete and confidential chat to take place away from prying ears. It also allowed the guest speaker to mingle with the councillors to give them individual advice and encouragement. The speaker and Steve got on like a house on fire. He cajoled Steve into considering standing for parliament as he came across as a straight-talking honest man:

"It did not matter which party you were currently a

member of as any major party would always find a safe seat for the right person. A person's past affiliations, upbringing or personal behaviour were irrelevant. Political parties required amiable and pragmatic parliamentarians to get policies implemented. It was rare for an outspoken disliked parliamentarian to get consensus. A photogenic poker-faced realist made the ideal candidate. Help would be given to make you look the part, whether that was elocution lessons to sound authentic, acting lessons to appear expressive and forthright or being surrounded by the right speechwriters."

"Play the game correctly and success would come. The prestige of being a parliamentarian brought rich rewards."

"Just look at me, all you see did glitter with gold. This seminar earned one hundred thousand for my consultancy. Always remember, the system funnelled everyone down the same path where integrity gave way to pragmatism: raw ingredients in and the same quality of package goods out at the other end. On the way through the grinder, you had to ensure the blame for any shit did not spread on you and to remember to reward not only loyal timeservers but also the disaffected as well to encourage them to remain silent. Parliamentary committees, quangos and the House of Lords were full of such people."

As the guest speaker made his way among fellow councillors, Steve had no choice but to hear some

insights of the opinion of our leaders regarding the
relationship between politicians and the public. In the
end, the public got what it deserved, as it ridiculously
demanded straightforward explanations to complex
interrelated fundamental problems faced by a modern
state. They unrealistically expected their leaders to
instantly know the solutions to all unexpected
problems. They applied required virtues to leaders
that did not exist in real life. The indigestible truth
was that no one was perfect. The majority of people in
the country personalised everything and were unable
to comprehend the big picture. Freedom was not their
prime concern; only the preservation of their own
little bubbles aroused them. One thing in common
was at the root of this goal. They all based their
personal security on the trustworthiness of money, it
kept them working and pacified. However, no state
working in isolation could guarantee a stable and
reliable currency. The global free market economy due
to competition between stock markets was by its
nature unregulated and competitive: a battle for
supremacy. It was a fallacy to expect the consolation
of a safe haven in old age after decades of toiling. The
role of modern political leaders was to protect society
against itself by hiding the harsh realities of life. Only
the rich could afford the luxury of being openly candid
and honest. The secret was to get your propaganda
out first to deny the truth of others. Successful
politicians had to be chameleons to appear all things
to all people. To the people at home they were
guardians and to the rest of the world they were
global leaders building bridges between different
cultures to enable trade by encouraging the rich to
invest money here. The only way to do this was to lie

successfully. Everyone lies and for some it was only a matter of choosing the right philosophy to attempt to justify the rights and the wrongs. Ordinary people lie to protect their egos or their families. Politicians were the emulation of society, no better and no worse. Always remember, with civic duty came responsibility, so lying was on a larger scale. The secret was to believe the lie when saying it rather than try justifying it afterwards. The key role of the state was to give the illusion of security and stability in a disordered brutal world. The public demanded reassurance and justification for the life choices provided to them. It was paramount to maintain a purpose for following society's conventions otherwise there would be chaos on the streets. The fact was that life was about the survival of the fittest and lying helped to preserve western values against people who hated us. The West was literally on a war footing as the means to cause mass destruction was in easy reach of all and sundry. To guarantee outcomes for the greater good casualties had to be taken today. Beyond the headlines, all great political leaders of the past had to get their hands dirty to safeguard our way of life. Beneath the veneer of civilised values, macho steel stopped rivals from pulling everything down. It was not a job for the worrier or the paranoid.

Steve had known himself to unexpectedly whistle on some occasions but never to laugh aloud as he just did. Maybe it was due to not being accustomed to the effect of the uppers that were supplied to him, but for the first time in his life, self-doubt made him reflect on whether he could pull off such a stunt. To rationally convince yourself to be the guardian of the

people and to be able to maintain a persona
purporting such righteousness would be impossible for
him to bear. He would rather just remain honestly
indifferent to the problems of others. He also thought
that it was lucky that the Vatican declared Jansenism
as heresy or this guest speaker would be spending a
long time in perdition while he waited for redemption
for his unconfessed sins. On parting, the former
statesman handed out pamphlets to the assembled
guests highlighting the services that his own
consultancy had to offer.

The last event in the afternoon was an individual
session to meet the team of advisors assigned to each
councillor to help package together the arguments for
supporting the development throughout the upcoming
consultation phase. Telephone numbers were swopped
to allow instant access to speechwriters to give the
best replies to unforeseen questions and any
forthcoming challenging interviews. In the case for
Steve, this involved exploring all the environmental
angles with ecological integrity, social and economic
justice, with respect and care for the community at
the forefront of the arguments used to sell the
development. The development would not only ensure
that local fauna and flora were not disturbed during
the development of the marina but ecological research
teams would be sponsored to monitor the environment
to determine the best ways of maintaining biological
diversity. There were also health benefits due to the
creation of walkways, cycling tracks and sports
facilities. All the values and principles required to
guarantee a sustainable future along with promises to
invest in eco-technologies to build a complex that

would be environmentally friendly while at the same time protect the town from the adverse effects of global warming. The development would not only protect the seafront from tidal surges and create hospitality jobs; it would also help to regenerate the commercial centre by enticing clean energy companies into the area to work on research projects around the marina. These projects would investigate the use of sustainable and renewable materials concerning the use of tidal and wind power, solar energy and heat pumps, building insulation and air conditioning, and photoelectric controls to manage energy usage.

The only real concern for the marketing team was how to show Steve their gratitude for his promised support. Looking at his background, they could not find any subtle way of rewarding him. He had no recognised children to get through their schooling years; he had no interest in acquiring season tickets for corporate boxes at the theatre or major sports events. The lack of strong political allegiance meant he would not appreciate financial donations to his party. In the end, they gave his charity the maximum amount of legal funding allowed and engineered a phone call from the hotel to inform him that he had accidentally left his money porch in his bedroom.

Steve's last action that day before catching a homeward train was to drop the pamphlet provided by the ex-statesman into the begging bowl of an old Roma woman outside the railway station. On reflection, he realised that the godfathers of this ubiquitous enterprise required no help in getting worldwide recognition of this enterprise's brand or advice on how to improve their business model. They already knew their core market and had the right skills balance within its staff to have a globally recognised standardised product. In fact, staff could be quickly deployed anywhere without the need for costly training or significant change in their work practices to comply with cultural differences. The core values of the organisation were clear and simple while its uncomplicated command and control structure quickly and unambiguously fed down directives. Dismissal of errant or non-performing staff did not involve costly bureaucratic procedures. Staff were shipped out in containers then returned home by getting free flights after declaring themselves as illegal migrants. The bosses of this enterprise had probably created the best business solution for today's demanding global market.

Back in Hayes-by-the-Sea, the news of a consortium wishing to develop the old harbour area had the expected mixed response. After several heated council debates with several referrals to committees, the council agreed to accept the invite to the Emirates to see in practice how they built internationally renowned marinas. As expected, a member from each party would make up the delegation. Julia was dissuaded from wishing to be considered, as the presence of a woman could make access to all areas difficult. Instead, she emphasised to Steve the importance of highlighting human right issues, social and economic justice and, of course, gender concerns like the subordination of women and the criminalisation of homosexuality. There must be visible signs that the Emirates seriously honoured their international commitments to spread democracy and they showed a nonviolent attitude to all ethnic groups.

The excited delegation packed their bags and headed out to the Arabian Gulf. The organised tours included visits to the Burj al Arab hotel, the Yas Marina, and Masdar City. Burj al Arab was designed to be iconic: a symbolic statement of the intention of the region to be seen as a dynamic place to visit and to do business. The one hundred eighty-metre-tall structure resembled the sail of a dhow, a type of Arabian vessel. Like the proposed hotel, it rested on an artificial island and its realisation required complex engineering feats. Yas Marina had over two hundred berths catering for boats from eight to one hundred and fifty metres with charter boats available for private and shared cruises. The marina had vibrant dining, many lifestyle choices, fitness centres, spas, aquariums and other entertainment facilities. Large terraces with panoramic views of the marina and a pedestrian promenade linking the whole complex together created an exclusive luxurious feel. Masdar City was a modern Arabian city that was in tune with its surroundings and was very friendly to pedestrians and cyclists. It was a model for sustainable urban development. The town planners were seeking to create a commercially viable development that delivered the highest quality living and working environment with the lowest possible ecological footprint, a hub for developing and testing renewable energy and clean technologies by encouraging companies to locate there; a place where costs did not matter allowing eco-conscious businesses to thrive and innovation to flourish.

At the end of their visit, a prince invited the delegation to a palace near the coast for lunch. One of the roles of this prince was to travel the globe looking for opportunities to invest some of the royal family's surplus wealth in ventures, which would increase their influence by nurturing friendships with powerbrokers while at the same time establish safe foreign domiciles. Foreign servants led them to their own guest room to freshen up before the official reception. The servants remained on hand to receive any instructions as the guests refreshed themselves. This highly secured compound had many guest rooms with everything that anyone would ever require, linked to elegant corridors with portraits of the royal family that led to large open planned lounges and TV rooms. These broad rooms had glass walls that opened up to a veranda given fantastic views of the desert, a planted grove of date palms, the distant beach and a swimming pool below.

This palace was only used to entertain foreign visitors, chiefly, statesmen, bankers and land developers looking for capital. Wives and children resided further inland in a zone prohibited to non-believing western eyes. The prince welcomed them inviting them for the next couple of hours to treat his abode as their own. After some alcoholic drinks, they sat down to a lunch that the Savoy hotel would have been very happy to serve. This prince re-iterated the importance of the friendship between their two great countries and then highlighted the United Arab Emirates' rapid economic growth and rising international profile. Mentioned the billions of dollars spent on infrastructure to put them at the cutting edge of architectural design. At the end of the reception, gifts were handed out to the delegates as a token to remember their visit to his humble country. Steve found the experience unnecessarily smarmy and patronising but nonetheless he took the gift anyway.

No one mentioned human rights, the lack of progress of the expansion of democracy or the strict adherence to Sharia law that demanded the execution by stoning of homosexuals, apostates and adulterers. Poor labour laws which effectively meant modern-day slavery. If reported back home issues of domestic worker abuse, in particular, sexual exploitation of female servants, would be of interest to unions and feminists. The most memorable incident for Steve was to observe the brusque arrest of a western bar manager in one of the hotels they resided: the manager had earlier refused to serve alcohol to an inebriated Arab who gate crashed a private karaoke.

ART FOR HIS SAKE

After abandoning his old life in Italy, Steve initially returned to Railhead to look up Jason, in the hope of finding a quiet spot to recoup from travelling before moving on. After just several days, he found that this first stop was a bad mistake as either he had grown too big for the town or it had shrunk. The place was just too dull, Jason appeared crankier, tiresome, and more highly strung since they last met. He seemed to spiral out of control over silly pointless incidents; he was now just too madly wrapped up in himself. The only joy Steve got was taking some cash that Jason had left lying around to spend it at a nearby Thai massage parlour that a conversation in a local pub informed him did extras when asked. Although he would not consciously concede it the time spent back in suburbia did at least allow him to readjust to the different sounds and to cramp city living, especially so in the crowded south.

The next stop took him up town where he made the re-acquaintance of some down on their luck artists from the old collective who informed him that the council sponsored communal studio had closed down. Most of the ex-members had spread their wings to go off in various directions to find the next big happening. Steve soon quickly realised that up town living would eat up his money unless he went back to a more frugal lifestyle, squatted and hoped for things to improve. This definitely did not appeal so he made the journey south to the coast where some of the guys said was attracting attention for the place to be.

The designated seaside town was always a well-known spot for getting away from the bustle of up town. It had culture and candyfloss, a long Victorian pier and a hotchpotch of architecture mainly reflecting late Georgian through to Victorian styles. It had always attracted actors and artists to make their homes there as well as being a venue for adulterous weekends and drunken beach fights. It was usually the first place visited on the south coast by day-trippers from up town. Its lanes were full of shops and lively bars. Most artisan shops did not have to make a profit but were purely the playthings of the owners. In more recent times, the town had become a powerful magnet that attracted dynamic like-minded people determined to carve out their own way of life, a place that overtly tolerated most things, a place where the avant-garde was becoming expected. It had adopted a tolerant European attitude. It had become the home of the well to do, the sexually adventurous, the transgender, gay and lesbian communities. Any type of drug was flagrantly available with the unexpected expected. This would be the first place in the country where the local police held hands as they walked the beat.

Alfredo came to life on the coast as Steve went into
hiding in case his whereabouts filtered back to
interested parties in Italy. Alfredo received welfare
and a national insurance number when local
unsuspecting benefit office staff happily accepted his
forged birth certificate and passport and registered
him as looking for work. He wandered around the
right pubs to make the acquaintance of gregarious
socialisers. Landing on his feet by meeting prosperous
people of leisure who enjoyed good drinking company
and were happy to spend money rather than hoard it,
revived Steve's acquaintance with good easy living.
He loved the way the well-off went down paths that
the less fortunate never travelled. In particular, he
enjoyed the company of a free-spending drinking
companion who could only receive a large monthly
allowance from a managed trust fund if he could prove
to be trying to forge his own living rather than just
spending the hard-earned family fortune. His father
thought he was being smart when he wrote his will
with the clear intent of stopping his son from
throwing away the amassed fortune. Unfortunately,
his specified requirements were not tight enough nor
envisaged changing work practices as his wily son just
created a job with the minimum possible working
hours to receive his monthly cheque from the
solicitors managing the trust fund. In principle, he
was a freelance financial consultant for another
friend's business but in reality, never did anything.
Instead, now with the help of Steve, he spent most of
his time drinking and smoking joints.

Later, his false identification papers then helped him
get a EU foreign student grant for full-time

attendance at the local Art College. During the induction week for foreign students, he met the young Mi-Cha, freshly off the plane from Korea, friendless, in a strange culture, and open to corruption. She wanted more than just to exist so she pestered her parents to allow her to expand her experience by finishing her education abroad. The new surroundings and life as a student in a liberal western environment thrilled her. It lived up to expectations. The antics and the feeling of entitlement of local students did initially overwhelm her. Nothing considered absurd as she entered a can do as you want world. The authorities remained indifferent to your morals so long as no serious criminal laws were broken.

Easy friendships developed among small gatherings where the consumption of alcohol, cannabis and cocaine heightened the emotions and removed inhibitions. Once Steve knew the full extent of the financial background of her family back in Korea, his attention at these gatherings was concentrated on Mi-Cha. Her poor tolerance to the after effects of induced highs resulted in prolonged anxiety and paranoia attacks that Steve found amusing. Morphine based substances were dismissed out of hand due to strong connotations with council housing scheme deprivation. Experimentation in other drugs like ecstasy, crack, meow meow and khat never really caught on as the happy mix of joints and snorted coke suited their gatherings better, ultimately considered trendier and higher class than the lowbrow alternatives. With the use of skunk and his normal direct approach that appealed to her sense of rebellion, desire to be shocked and to be seen as someone special, Steve managed to detach Mi-Cha from the pack.

The course modules followed by Steve essentially focused on modern trends such as installation art. Postmodern art was now a 3D experience where all types of media and material combined to immerse the viewer within an artificially created shell to change perception, stir emotions and with any luck alter opinions. The re-use of everyday discarded industrial and domestic waste expressed individualism: turning rubbish into eye-catching thought-provoking sculptures to make the masses think about the impact of their waste on the local environment and the rest of the world. Discussions abound on how art should be used to express feminist, sexual and cultural politics. Art had its part to play in society. Its voice had to be heard. It forced people to try to make sense of modern life. It was beautiful, emotive and complex, and a powerful tool to explain what was happening.

The appreciation of low art was here to stay, the more mundane the materials used or the setting, the more inspirational its message and greater reception from the art world. Graffiti, once considered as vandalism and costly to the ratepayer, was now glorified by the art establishment with the spray painter declared an urban hero, using his skills to claw his or her way out of poverty to be allowed to sit at the table of well-educated art experts. The most basic of disfranchised acts available to the disenfranchised youth recognised as a symbol of rebellion. Consequently, the lecturers encouraged students to take to the streets to conduct off the cuff theatrical performances or displays of short-lived art works. Art was for the masses, had to be seen outside galleries, and it had to be part of and reflect society not stand outside it. They must not think that everything had been done and there was nothing new out there. Life did not come to them: they had to go to it. They had to confront the norm to express their right to free expression. Become vibrant and take ownership of the streets. Mediums like street dance freed the mind. Was a naked rambler an eccentric fool, a persistent common decency offender or a naturist pioneer expressing the right to keep faith to his principles?

Steve remained indifferent to any hint of political or social considerations in art. He only actually enjoyed attending history lectures on the evolution of modern art as it covered periods and artists that he had tried imitating when part of the art collective up town. All the movements attempted in the own way to use shapes and colour to get closer to the true physical nature of objects and beings. These lectures gave him some appreciation of the theory behind their works and new vocabulary to impress the uninitiated. The various stages of cubism and the cult status of Pablo Picasso wetted his lips. Picasso had a shared recognition with Georges Braque for bringing to the world Analytic Cubism, which dissected objects and re-shaped them on canvas with the use of monochrome brownish and neutral colours. Synthetic Cubism marked the arrival of collage with cut paper fragments from mass production sources pasted into compositions. Celebrities and the greats of high culture all flocked to Picasso's studio to glaze upon the greatest artist of that time. The artist's celebrated sexual potency fascinated Steve. Furiously erotic, a Minotaur whose leitmotif was depicting his copious collection of emotionally flawed young mistresses, portraying them beyond the real to express his torrid tortured love. It emphasised the fact that you could get away with anything in society if deemed above the pact. Coerced morals did not apply to the greats. No one called them dirty old men. Pop art born up town was the start of the recognition of the aestheticism found in consumerism. It was the start of the modern trend to mirror contemporary society. Stripping art to its bare essentials also had attracted Steve's attention, as it seemed so easy to replicate. The lectures in minimalism compared Western European geometrical abstractions to the succinct clear lines that flowed through North American works. Nowadays, abstraction and minimalism were at the heart of the all-embracing branding industry as it helps convey an immediate eye-catching message to the masses. Art had now moved on.

Mi-Cha found the culture of the country alluring and immediately fell in love with the ubiquitous neo-Gothic. A movement with a long history that had a lasting influence on the rest of the world as it spread around the old empire. Where there was light, darkness soon followed. The blood-sucking Dracula came from abroad to exploit the country by using its infrastructure to quickly get around to gather up converts to enhance his harem and quench his thirst. He was the devil in everyday clothes that could melt the heart of any woman. Everything came at a price. Vampires were not just supernatural creatures looking for an excitable naïve maiden. They were also part of the machine that governed commerce, daily life and manipulated fears. The story of the vampire parodied industrialisation, as craft men turned into zombie wage slaves and wives became lured adulteresses consuming mass-produced goods. Nowadays, the Internet and high street were the high altars of capitalism, where buying was deemed more important than sex. Pagans worshipped their gods with displays of orgies, these new devotees trooped around the shops demanding more and more consumption, pure exploitation of primeval instincts found in women.

The Enlightenment may have dismissed religion with the devil along with it but human society still refused to let them go. In the past, Karl Marx, John Ruskin and William Morris were part of the Victorian Gothic revival against the evils of industrialisation and mass production. It was a movement for the people. Its greatest architect was Augustus Welby Northmore Pugin with its art championed by the Pre-Raphaelites. It had a moral and philosophical appeal expressed by men of literature. They promoted collectivism and art nouveau to challenge the anti-human invasion by the emerging global commerce. Gothic art had a perpetual appeal; always attracting the young with each generation re-inventing it to suit their own needs and beliefs. In modern times, the young refused to give up on the wearing of black and suspecting that corruption tarnished every adult. They resisted as long as possible the pressures to sell their souls and become fully-fledged members of humanity. Their representation of vampires and concubines portrayed a young sexy dynamic image.

They were anti-heroes in slim well-cut clothing ready to fight for the right to survive, to endure the pains of forbidden love or to love whom they desired. Modern Gothic was everywhere: readers loved it, its music enticed many millions around the world, magazines used it to sell issues and galleries were full of its imaginary. Fashion designers and artists were inspired by it. Tattooists made their living from it. Fantasy and science fiction movies were essentially at heart Gothic genres where attractive or grotesque aliens wanted to be invited into your domain for despicable and destructive reasons.

Mi-Cha took to the wearing Gothic tee shirts and jewellery as her symbols of freedom. All her early artistic endeavours had a kernel of Gothicism. She was naturally creative and a good learner. She rebelled against the modern world by preferring craft skills like ceramics and needlework to the *en vogue* video and electronic art productions. She loved visiting ruins and Gothic cathedrals. She insisted on visiting Whitby to see the landing spot of the creature and to get her picture taken while posing on fallen gravestones in the prominently placed old abandoned abbey grounds. Afterwards, a distinctive feature of her attire from that visit was a tight-fitting jet Coptic cross necklace that perfectly matched the colour of her hair.

Late night social occasions were fun times as they debated anything under the sun or played with the toys of the occult. If the development of language allowed humans to evolve mechanisms for conscious thinking then do animals by their nature only have instinctive mental processes, they possess an ID but no ego? That sophistry was a conscious trick allowing man's ego to justify self-interest or even heinous acts; acts not observed in the animal kingdom? The only philosophical argument worth adhering was Schopenhauer's thirty-eight stratagems? They performed incantations to prevent any of them from suffering penury or to inflict terrible diseases on adversaries; group séances lead to contact with the spirit world; Ouija board sessions to communicate with earthbound trapped entities like ghosts and the use of the tarot to give guidance on important questions and to predict the future. Although never taken too seriously, frights and screams of delight were infectious among all those present. There was no serious thought in their minds of evil forces using the fun seekers' channelling to the spiritual world to take control of their souls or steal them. Just in case, they did follow the guidelines to vanquish lingering unannounced malevolent spirits before sessions ended, and ensured that invited spirit guides knew they were only temporary guests who had to depart in peace to their own domain leaving them unmolested. Tarot card readings also excited their imaginations and aroused fears. In the beginning, they experimented with a simple one-card draw to unravel the answers to straightforward phrased questions. When questions were asked about the sitters' personalities, Steve's first ever card was the King of Wands while Mi-Cha pulled out the Page of Cups. This effectively summed up the power play of their future together. They then moved on to multiple card readings using the Celtic cross ten-card layout. Allowing them to not only predict the outcome to various posed questions but also obtain indications of how events would unravel.

Mi-Cha had barely unpacked her belongings in the student hostel before Steve whisked her off to share a flat rented in her name. He had persuaded her that she had to live in the community if she wanted to understand the psyche of the nation. Meet other people to experience life away from college. She became a young foreign woman propelled into a world of adults as she socialised with Steve and his drinking companions. Over time, Steve gradually dictated his preferences on her as the couple settled down to an existence together. Mi-Cha got used to being the means that enabled Steve to pursue his own undertakings. Courtesy of her father's money, the couple had many long weekends away in all the exciting capitals of Europe. They indulged themselves when visiting all the renowned museums and art galleries. The highlight was Berlin, the role model of any city that wanted to create an avant-garde bastion. The eroticism of Berlin's punk and Goth culture naturally excited the Korean. Decadence was in its roots. It had a lively young art scene nurtured by the open-mindedness of the authorities. There was a vibrant cultural and social life, abundant street theatres, and daring transvestite shows. It was the historic centre of the European sex trade, a city populated by liberally-minded people tolerant of nudity and public sex in their municipal parks. Their visit unintentionally coincided with Fetish Week celebrations in this capital. Latex and leather events brought people from all over the world to the streets and clubs. The spellbinding displays of avant-garde bondage and fetish acts in a city notorious for its dark austere past stimulated them. It was the icing on the cake. Foreplay for the couple over that weekend involved hot wax dipping and good old fashion over the knee spanking.

A gregarious art teacher one night befriended Steve in the student bar after noticing a pack of tarot cards in his open bag. He was a youngish forty-year-old with the gaunt complexion of a vegetarian. The academic was a well-groomed man, clean shaved with short tidy hair. He wore his customary uniform of corduroy jeans, a short sleeve shirt under a fashionable short lapelled two-buttoned suede jacket. The days of dishevelled lecturers with bedraggled hair and beards giving off the odour of booze mingled with that from cigarettes were long gone. This wage earner perpetually wondered for how much longer he could teach a new generation of young want to be artists before he was labelled as being part of the old establishment and irrelevant. This feeling was exasperated by the fact that he taught about the latest trends in art and not historic art. The lecturer was envious of Steve's return to college as a mature student because his worldly wisdom would stand out as a beacon to impressible young females. The man took it upon himself to expand Steve's knowledge and understanding of the occult.

Steve was suspicious when this lecturer discussed alternative beliefs and their importance. However, he gave him the benefit of the doubt as he came across earnest rather than pretentious or sinister, sounding new age than anything as dangerous as being associated with gun touting mid-west American survivalists or as serious-minded as the Scientologists or as unwavering as the Animal Rights activists. Steve let him expostulate reasons why cults still persisted in the modern world. Despite the general censoriousness, alternative beliefs served a purpose; they stopped the mainstream faiths from becoming complacent, keeping them on their toes. In addition, the presence of many views was a sign of social awareness and dynamism. They allowed enlightened individuals to find a different way. Most anthropology theories and other reflections on the past only had historical relevance to give us some basic idea of the thoughts that pre-occupied the past and could not really reflect actual life back then. In truth, their societies were just as complex as our own. Their leaders were just as intelligent and manipulative as ours. They well understood the mechanics of their own culture. Primitives always reacted to the unknown by presuming the existence of beings or forces that were superior to them. The primitive magic men were not ignorant of casual connections, they knew that rites on their own would not vanquish their enemies or cause crops to flourish. The purpose of rites was to bring the tribe together to forge unity and prepare for the challenge ahead. Nevertheless, words and customs were important, as psychological barriers were always the hardest to break down. The ritual of the scapegoat to carry sins out into the wilderness in *Leviticus,* for example, would be a symbolic removal of sins not actual. All groups used rhetoric to proclaim their version of the truth. They all have their rituals and canons to follow. Rhetoric was just a search for solutions to problems. Many religions took a grain of truth or tribal belief then extrapolated it to their own ends. Tradition was a rich mix of history, myth, accepted truths and the propaganda of winners. Lancelot was the invention of the conquering Normans to humiliate the Saxons by cuckolding the legendary king. Before this defamation, Perceval of the Grail was the leading knight who championed the king's one nation vision. If people did not safeguard their heritage, others would misuse it for their own benefit.

Being different from convention always attracted suspicion with their meetings called cults to differentiate them from accepted truths and to denigrate them. State tolerance of cults occurred only if their teachings did not preach the breaking of secular laws but there was disdain from mainstream religions that provoked strong reaction and resistance to them. Outsiders took a prejudicial stance claiming that followers of cults were being brainwashed to lose their autonomy through deception, all kinds of abuse and deprivations. The assumption was that all members of the cult were under direct manipulation of their all-powerful leader. He trapped people who were weak and searching for meaning. New members probed for psychological weaknesses to enable the shattering of their fragile egos so that the cult could rebuild them to be subservient to its will. Worn down, they became blind and de-sensitised to the lamentations of the outside world. The faith of the initiated follower was severely tested to determine their loyalty. Upon full membership to a cult, family and friends were abandoned and freedom lost. The declared prophets of the cult perceived the past, present and future simultaneously by predicting events just after they happened so they could never be wrong. There was no free will. The leader was a charlatan who nefariously achieved financial and sexual gains. Worse still some preached a doomsday scenario to provoke terrible murderous group acts.

On the other hand, alternative thinkers believed their teachings would help followers cope better with the turmoils that occurred in life, and of those turmoils, that they predicted would soon happen. They too would point out the deceptions seen in life to explain how people were corralled into thinking and believing the same propagated false truths. Followers would say that they have taken a different path and seen the light. They would proclaim to now think with their heart and trust themselves to believe there was a better way to live. Anger dissipated to liberate their spirit. They had purged themselves of hate to allow the generation of trust. The way mainstream society existed declared as false and unnatural, harmful to the environment and other creatures. The established powers maligned them because they threatened their control.

Despite condemnation, alternative groups were not all the same. Some were political and others' indifferent to the machinations of the State and Church. In addition, time and changing events altered the public perception of people who wanted to challenge mainstream thinking. Greenpeace were once considered an outlaw organisation, full of anarchists who hated the country of their birth. Now their views were sought after at every opportunity by the news media. Some groups had roots extending back to a distant indigenous past when matriarchal societies existed in a time when man's fate was intertwined with nature. The landscape still bears their mark while the Christian Church stole their festival days. The people of the mist in time believed in Goddesses along with the power of the dead to influence future actions. They ruled this land until the Roman imperialist male God suppressed woman and nature. This alien religion gave man the right to do whatever he wanted with the planet and the rest of animal kingdom. Nowadays, the established order ridiculed and portrayed past rituals as hocus-pocus: fetish men who watched and encouraged witches to dance in the skins of slain young virgins; inducing trances and making ritual sacrifices to bring forth evil spirits to reap murder on the innocent. The truth of the matter, the old ways gave the elderly a place in the heart of the community. Knowledge of nature allowed administration of health given herbal potions to the sick, created hearty tasty meals and flavoured drinks for feast days. Spring and harvest festivals brought the young from the surrounding areas together to allow the gene pool to remain healthy and strong. Being righteous and having good habits made you dull; fun was required to liven you up, and paganism was synonymous with fun. The lecturer told him to come along to the Druids bar in town one night if he was interested in learning more about the occult and its relevance to the art scene today. You also got good hashish there as well.

For a bit of fun, Steve duly trotted along one night, to see a bar he had previously heard about but never

visited. It had the reputation of being a novelty pub
with many macabre artefacts on display, a tourist pub
where the easy-going regulars were sociable to
strangers. When he entered the bar, Steve ordered an
unfiltered cider then stood at the bar. The pub itself
was worth a visit. Many stuffed cats, weasels, ferrets,
rabbits and all sorts of birds, bats and small vermin
along with voodoo and witchcraft related items and
imagery covered the walls and ceiling. The counter,
wall panelling, flooring, tables and benches all
rustically carved from a dark wood that smelled as if
lacquered with some secret herb infused resin. The
older regulars, who knew best, would say that the
surrounds had been impregnated with dragon's blood.
Sitting was discretely arranged in little nooks and
crannies, only large enough for small isolated groups
of four or five. The clientele looked comfortable in
their surroundings and the drinks on offer reflected
their traditional tastes. A drinker from the turn of the
last century would have recognised all the drinks on
offer. The hand pumps had several different ciders
and strong amber bitters. The labels on the bottled
spirits in the gantry had many a well-known old
name. It was definitely not a bar for the young. There
was a complete absence of cocktail mixtures and
aftershock drinks. Golden ales and porter were only
available in bottles. As for alternative drinks for any
nominated car driver then they could forget it.

Apart from the Hammer Horror setting, nothing else
felt sinister. The overheard quiet conversations were
just the usual mundane nonsense, the low-key folk
music from a speaker was relaxing, and no one
appeared out of a puff of smoke. As Steve was

wondering where he would go for the next pint, his presence caught the eye of one of the chatting groups and before he knew it, he was encouraged to join them. Deep in the corner of a recess was the art lecturer, hidden in the shadows as if the light would turn him to dust. Sitting with him was a taxidermist, a mortician beautifier and a woman of independent means who declared herself a writer. He did not know this at the time but could have made a good guess at their professions by their manner and dress. The taxidermist was a chubby jolly fellow in his late forties, the beautician for the dead looked mid-thirties and uncomfortable when talking to the living. The writer was the oldest and most laidback of the group. She was probably early fifties and introduced herself as Maureen. Her baggy clothes on a filling out body reflected a cosy look. This woman came across as astute and full of understanding. You would not have been surprised if she said her occupation was that of a senior social worker. Her facial bone structure indicated that she had once been considered a beauty. Even in her later years, Steve would have gladly spent the night with her. However, physical features do not always reveal inflicted mental scars obtained on the way to maturity. Maureen did most of the talking when the lecturer told them that Steve was interested in the occult and was broadminded about learning more about its cultural heritage and how it related to modern living. A series of questions and answers lasted for a couple of hours. The glasses never seemed to empty. The focus of the conversation was on the various uses of herbs and pigments derived from different natural substances. They were keen enthusiasts of all things natural. It was a nice

casual chat with joints liberally passed about when
they ventured into the enclosed yard for a smoke. If
he had something more engaging to do, he probably
would have walked straight out of the pub that night,
dismissed them as a bunch of cranks, and never
bothered to return to it. However, he would return to
see them because drinking in company of oddballs
was fun.

When he dropped into the Druids some of the faces
would change, but the conversations remained similar
in nature. Although they could be a boring lot, they
were also generous with their drink and joints. He
had drunk in worse company than this. Eventually,
an invitation to go back to the townhouse of the writer
arrived. They sat in a front room dominated by a full-
size reproduction of the *Druids Bringing Home the
Mistletoe* by Henry and Hornel surrounded by a built-
in bookcase. The light oak of the shelving matched the
rich red and golden colours of this decorative painting.
A collaboration loved by the Victorian arts and craft
movement. Maureen had many books on the occult,
indigenous crafts, natural food foraging, and
homeopathy. Some of the books contained detailed
illustrations of old rites, ancient herbal recipes and
pictorial examples Gothic art found in churches and
country manors. She explained that magical religions
or neo-paganism were not about death or summoning
the devil. Paganism should not cause fear. It offered a
more common sense understanding of humanity's
need for spirituality. They were polytheistic faiths
that did not ignore the role of chance or misfortune
had on the direction that life could take. Miracles
were rarely worshipped in their ideology, unlike some

religions. Unusual natural events were taking to
mean something was wrong indicating they had to
change what they were doing; they had to amend
their ways to please nature. Each culture was free to
put their heritage at the centre of the pagan faith, to
choose their morals, afterlife beliefs and even sexual
orientation. It was open to anyone to derive what he
or she wanted.

When Maureen thought Steve was ready, she took
him down into the basement, which ran the full
length of the house. In the centre of the floor was the
pentagram within a circle with a basic element
portrayed at each tip: air, fire, water, earth and spirit.
Their symbol for balance and strength. The lighting
came from high wall-mounted fittings with alternate
red and yellow low voltage bulbs. An illuminated
Wicca Rede dominated the wall at the end of the room
that faced the main road. On the opposite side of the
room, an altar resided protected on either side by
standalone statues of the horned god and the mother
goddess. The coven's Book of Shadows was placed on
the altar along with candle and incense holders. On
the wall behind the altar, hung a large framed picture
depicting a ceremonial dagger with the pagan tree of
life in the background. To add to the mystic
atmosphere the other walls held antique witch's
scribes along with tapestries depicting idyllic peasant
activities. On the ceiling, four distinct murals
illustrated Imbolc, Beltane, Lughnasadh and
Samhain celebrations.

Maureen was the priestess of this coven. The coven
met at each full moon and during festivities for the

lesser solstices. The enactment of ancient rituals at full moons were important to them because the mother goddess was associated with the moon, and the druids derived their seasonal calendar by observing its phases. The statues of the gods were only the anthropomorphosis of cosmic forces; they did not believe they were actual entities demanding worship. She could never understand why gods of other faiths required continual worship and praise. It implied servitude or something even more sinister. This coven did not believe that another life was waiting for anyone after death. Instead, they believed we all came from the cosmos and would go back to it. We were all part of the whole.

The celebration of the four greater Sabbaths necessitated a more formal gathering with other covens at the ancestral home of the family who returned indigenous worship back to the region. The Skyclad was encouraged at these larger events where the high priestess and her cortege of lesser priestesses would instigate a full pagan ceremony in the old Brythonic tongue. Maureen expressed her view that the sights and sounds of these occasions would fascinate Steve. Although they are solemn festivals, the celebrations afterwards were spectacular and rich in pageantry. There he would see and recognise all the traditional imagery depicting the likes of the green man, the sun god and Merlin the magician. All in a grand neo-Gothic hall with blazing gas burners, adorned with decapitated Celtic stone heads as the sound of horns and pipes echoed all around. With cauldrons full of mead or fortified wines to help raise spirits, what was said and happened on these nights stayed there. Nonetheless, these nights were not just an invite for sexual promiscuity. The symbolism of pretend orgies and the nakedness expressed the healthy need to keep the tribe strong. Steve wondered how comfortable it would be to expose his well-fed rotund body and stumpy cock next to an all over tanned Adonis with a huge penis that invariably would be there. He would have to drink plenty of sacramental wine on these occasions.

Steve naturally joined the coven in the hope to gain favours from other followers in the way that the masons helped each other. The reason behind their interest in Steve became clearer when he was encouraged to bring younger elements of the Art College to them. The new convert's access to the young in a social setting was a perfect way of finding candidates suitable for initiation into their coven. The fact was the recruitment of younger members was becoming difficult for the ageing witches, whose numbers were dropping below the required level to run an independent and fully functioning coven. Up to the nineties getting young couples to engage in their activities was easier as some of them thought it was a good way of possibly meeting similar minded people for other more adventurous activities like wife swapping, which was all the rage back then. Nowadays, the Internet allowed a more anonymous way of satisfying extramarital needs. Simply put they had an antiquated image and it was difficult to find young worthy enough to be trained in their beliefs. The priestess believed that it was imperative that their amassed knowledge was passed on to suitably trained followers. Only young blood would safeguard the future of the coven. They had no young of their own, or if they did, they did not follow the faith of their parents. Books alone would not safeguard their traditions, preserve skills and retain a full understanding of the symbolism behind their rituals and canons. Actual experience was vital to engrain the knowledge meticulously collated from old manuscripts and folklore. An outsider reading their work would not fairly convey their intent. It would also be good to turn up at the greater Sabbaths with followers that gave the beautiful young things of the other covens a run for their money. They were fed up being the butt of the let it all hang out gags. They wanted Steve to be a conduit for enticing desirables to their meetings, to meet the priestess and understand the cultural importance of their activities. Unknown to Steve, they were already aware of Mi-Cha and saw her as a possible convert, and maybe a future priestess. The art lecturer knew of her aptitude to learn, her artistic abilities, and her interest in the occult. By going through Steve, they hoped to get Mi-Chi. Maureen interests were not completely holistic. She strongly believed in the importance of the female and the contribution her gender made to create a fair society. She saw in Mi-Cha someone who could take ownership of their Book of Shadows. Of course, Steve only saw something he could exploit and never considered the possibility that others were using him. In this neo-pagan coven, Maureen was determined to find a worthy female successor. Two opposing players both had their eyes on the same prize.

Mi-Cha happily accepted the invite to the coven and naturally took a liking to Maureen. Here was a motherless woman keen to help the youngster find her way. In her youth Maureen's looks and liberal upbringing designated her as a good lay for sexual opportunists to add to their list of conquests, as a result, she never had a lover who became a soul mate. She only ever came across chaff and not wheat as she navigated her youthful years, never to meet someone looking beyond the superficial. Someone that did not assume she was high maintenance. With talent came responsibility. No matter what happened she wanted Mi-Cha to develop a belief that she could take control of her own life and she hoped to straddle the good things in Western and Eastern cultures. She wanted to direct Mi-Cha onto a path that would give her the confidence to believe in herself, to broaden her mind to accept different views and question orthodoxy in all its forms; no matter if at the end of the day she rejected paganism or not. Maureen, of course, believed that the myths and parables of orthodox thinking were just painted colour, texture and virtual depth on a flat monochrome canvas. They hid or submerged the harsh facts about modern human societies and created contrite reasons that engendered ties for the masses to cling on to. For many, life had become a struggle to live up to non-achievable standards. A strong free will was required to stop life becoming predestined due to all these constrictions imposed by today's society. Asserting free will was the only real form of rebellion left for an individual, as it would take a catastrophe to end archaic rule, duplicitous political systems and self-perpetuating religious organisations.

The love of the subject matter and her patient manner

made Maureen an ideal teacher. They discussed Celtic
art all the way back to Hallstatt. The ancients knew
how to forge metal and minerals into great art. Their
culture had a sophisticated understanding of
symbolism, producing abstract designs of animal
forms intertwined with flowing vegetation. She even
took interest in Mi-Cha's own reading of Korean
spiritualism. Mi-Cha explained the Korean creation
myth where the heavenly king and holy mother ruled
by handing down earthly power through a female
lineage. Shamans connected the people to heaven in
the hope of good fortune through trance rituals. When
Mi-Cha pointed out her upbringing was Christian
talks focused on the Roman Church and Mary
Magdalene. How the early Celtic Church founded on
ascetic mystic contemplation was usurped by the rigid
rule-based Roman Church. Rustic religious dwellings
replaced by outlandish splendour with the cult of
relics kept in crypts. She pointed out how Mary
Magdalene's importance had been played down by the
mischievous general use of the name Mary in the New
Testament to de-individualise women and by the
edicts of medieval popes to encourage the branding of
her as a common prostitute. Her gospel conferred
mystic teachings that went against classical thinking.
An austere doctrine using Socratic connotations, and
rigid rule following to avoid sin and retribution that
permeates through the Old Testament. However, even
the authorised Bible could not hide her importance.
She was the only person to witness all of the key
events which Christianity is based on. The crucifixion,
the burial of Jesus, the guarding of the tomb and
reporting to the twelve disciples that Jesus had risen
again. She was the apostle to the apostles. The only

one who never denied knowing Jesus during the passion and kept her faith in his message. Her perceived sin was to spread a mystic message of enlightenment that aligned spirituality with the whole cosmos to create a completed human being capable of denying materialistic and selfish temptations, putting the capability to love and trust at the centre of its message. Jesus was not an ascetic prude but welcomed relationships so long as they followed the rules perpetually reformulated in pop songs: find someone to love, they love you, and remember to kiss often. Warning that without reciprocated love earthly relationships was like living with a corpse. Hearts resonate in partnership only when giving and receiving were in equal quantities.

Maureen continually emphasised the importance of the Book of Shadows. If humankind had to start again without complex technology then the information held in it would quickly allow a civilised nature-friendly society to rise from the ashes of burnt out electronics. It was their task to maintain and enlarge the book, keeping it up to date and safe for future generations. None of their texts alluded to death or violence in their rituals. Vegetal offerings celebrated life and the sharing of resources, not sacrificial killing to atone for human weakness or to enhance the achievement of desired outcomes. Grains in the form of cakes and porridge symbolised regrowth, strength and fertility.

Mi-Cha was, as foreseen, a good learner and comprehended the fundamentals behind the vast range of topics covered. By accentuating her positives, Maureen hoped to release Mi-Cha from her penchant for easily falling under the influence of dominant males, regardless of her intellectual superiority over them. The more Maureen came across Steve the more convinced she was that Mi-Cha could do better than a man completely lacking in any integrity; a man insusceptible to compassion, to apprehension, or to guilt. He made her skin crawl. Chemical castration would be her preferred solution to reduce his testosterone levels to neutralise his sexual forcefulness. She even instructed Mi-Cha on how to make potions to reduce male urges in the hope she would get the hint. Unfortunately, any hope of turning her into a strong freethinking woman was doomed to fail. It was not the right time in Mi-Cha's life to convince her to claim possession of herself. Her recalcitrant attraction to Steve was too strong. She remained uninterested in philosophical thought, political ideas or gender issues. A self-destructive craving along with heightened hormone levels permitted Steve to dominate her. She had a flair for the practical side of life but her personality stopped her from forging an ego with sufficient narcissism to stand alone in life. The only hope would be that in adult life Maureen's efforts would be remembered and appreciated by Mi-Cha, and used to her life back on track.

While training occupied Mi-Cha's time, Steve became better acquainted with the other members of the coven. They all had something to contribute to the survivalist's toolkit, which was their Book of Shadows. His eyebrows rose with curiosity when he ascertained what some of them did for an occupation. This was when he found out that John was a taxidermist and

Imogene worked at an undertaker. John said it was better to poison or gas the creature first as no blemishes should appear on the skin. The treated skin was stretched over a jointed artificial body with its cleaned skull attached to it, all adjusted until the mounted creature appeared lifelike. The eyes were just made of glass. The skinned carcass thrown away as it was not fit for human consumption. Nowadays, beginners could buy kits to get them started. Imogene explained her role was purely cosmetic. The body was stiff as a board once her part in the process was required. She could replicate the facial features easily enough if the bereaved gave her a photo with a good likeness of the deceased. It was not as if the deceased was going to complain about how she got the match. Although plain looking and built like a stick the childish giggling while elucidating her role gave Imogene some charm, which up to then was completely undetectable to Steve. Naturally, Steve was interested to see them both in action.

The taxidermist had his own workshop in an extended shed at the back of his garden so access to him was easy. Steve arranged to see the transformation of a former beloved pet. While he watched John, it struck him how some people find work that suits them. John's little bright eyes became intense as his small nimble hands scraped and cleaned the skin of the animal in front of him. The economy and simplicity of his actions betrayed the skill required to obtain perfect results. Steve revealed some of his own experiences of skinning and butchering animals in Italy. Admitting his nearest neighbour supervised him and was not completely impressed with his efforts.

The difficulty in observing the beautifier was resolved by gaining temporary employment at the funeral parlour over the winter break when demand picked up due to flu epidemics, the rise in suicides, domestic murders and deaths due to loneliness that accompanied the festive period. From an artistic viewpoint, it would be good experience to see the many faces and stages of decay so that any naturalistic representation would be realistic. When he first heard about the opportunity to help around the undertaker, his initial thought was the desire to create a photo collage of the deceased for that year's college art project. He had even fantasised about borrowing the dead to place them on park seats dedicated to the memory of others gone before them. In the end, the impracticality of the idea curtailed all his initial intentions.

First, he had to negotiate an interview with the funeral director to show that he had the stomach for the work. This involved an explanation of the work done behind the scenes, a health and safety lecture and a tour of the facilities. Preparation for the funeral service began when the corpse came from the hospital or the police morgue. Temperature control preserved a corpse for weeks. The embalming process performed by a mortician prevented the spread of disease and allowed the corpse to be presentable until after the funeral. The naked corpse, placed on a tilted mortuary table with draining groves, with the head elevated by a block was washed in disinfectant and germicidal solutions. The mortician then, if required, worked and massaged the arms and legs to relieve rigor mortis to get the body into the correct position. Injection of embalming chemicals into the carotid artery displaced blood and interstitial fluids, expelling them through the right jugular vein. This was called drainage. Cavity embalming replaced internal fluids inside the body using an aspirator and trocar. The mortician made a small incision just above the navel to ease the passage of a trocar into the chest and stomach cavities. This punctured the hollow organs to permit the suction of their contents. Solutions containing formaldehyde would then fill the created cavities. Surface embalming occurred to preserve and restore areas directly on the skin's surface when there was damage due to the cause of death, accidents or decomposition. Afterwards, the corpse was stitched closed and washed, including shampooing the hair. Facial hair, which could interfere with makeup application, was shaved. A typical embalmment took several hours to complete. The repair of a corpse after an autopsy or received remains of a donor took longer. The embalmed corpse would be dressed in clothes delivered by a family member. After that, the corpse was set in the casket and the beautician styled the hair and makeup for viewing by family and friends.

The trocar functioned as a portal for subsequent manipulation by other instruments. It also allowed the escape of the build-up of gases from decomposing organs or bloating. It was first used in Europe in the eighteenth-century after centuries of royal mourners having to put up with exploding dead monarchs due to their bodies being displayed in their open caskets for too long. This last titbit was meant to defuse the solemnity of their tasks by bringing in a bit of humour. Forewarned Steve appeared suitably austere and prosaic throughout the interview. He showed no sign of squeamishness during the tour. The urgency in getting help and the unavailability of the usual late standby forced the funeral director to make a quick decision to employ Steve to do the dog work. This would relieve some of the pressure on the qualified morticians, allowing them to spend more time on working through the backlog of waiting deceased.

It was like a factory line behind the scenes as old and young arrived for preparation to the afterlife. The corpses were put in cold storage until the bereaved families decided on the funeral arrangements. Steve ensured bottles were full; the area kept sterile and helped to unload and store corpses as they arrived in a plain blue van. He watched all the processes with interest as his nasals got used to the stanch of the embalming chemicals and putrefied waste. He could only watch the early embalming processes from afar due to the explained health and safety measures. The morticians in their green plastic gowns, masks and gloves worked away on two stabs parallel to each other. A casket would be wheeled in when embalmment was completed and taken to the viewing room where Imogene would apply the final touches. He could stand next to Imogene and chat to her as she worked her magic. The only days off for the crew were Christmas and Boxing Day. On Christmas Eve, they shared a drink in the morgue before going their separate ways. The presence of funeral staff in a local pub that night would not be appreciated.

Steve worked on Imogene to get him into the morgue on Boxing Day so that he could satisfy his curiosity. He had taken her out for a drink on several occasions and she had not scorned his advances. He snared her without much effort. She possessed a set of work keys and knew the code for the alarm. In the past, she had returned alone to the funeral parlour to diligently finish rushed jobs. They meet outside the staff entrance, and quietly entered the still and eerie premises; the added chill from no business activity for several days hit them immediately. Steve intended to satisfy a morbid lust for necrophilia. They wandered into the morgue, pulled opened the cabinets to look at the latest arrivals. He selected a youngish woman for the task. Imogene rightly pointed out it would be rather messy if he attempted to desecrate an untreated corpse. It would also be spotted when the mortician saw the body whereas desecration of an already embalmed corpse would not be detected. Reluctantly he conceded and viewed some finished articles awaiting their funeral service. The choice was limited and not that appealing but he was committed to the task. A deceased female pensioner was the unlucky object for violation. Steve finally had a sexual partner with the same emotional affections as himself. Unfortunately for Steve, the cold air had a detrimental effect on the proposed act, causing Steve extreme difficulty in raising the means to penetrate the deceased. The deceased, due to rigor mortis, was also exceeding unwilling to yield. In the end, Imogene had to get down on her knees to arouse him. In the absence of a speculum, a trocar was used to ply open the anus, after an attempt to create a cavity in the corpse's vagina had failed. The completion of the disgusting act involved large quantities of Vaseline, and Imogene making a three-some.

The esbats bored Steve. They were too academic and lacked spontaneity. He just did not understand the desire to prepare for doomsday instead of just partying now if you thought life was going to drastically change in the near future. The major Sabbaths brought more joy. They were surprisingly well-organised affairs, very middle class. The night started with the coven getting on a hired bus to head out to a Victorian Gothic manor house where about one hundred followers of various persuasions all met to partake in a night of frolics. Rumour had it, the manor had a large collection of sorcery rarities and curiosities, and that not in far-off past black masses were performed in all seriousness in an attempt to gain esoteric meaning. Sceptics condemned these antics as the actions of degenerates; libertines looking to justify lewd behaviour, sadism, unbridled debauchery and gratuitous sexual acts; people with too much time on their hands and in a position of influence to get away with amoral mischief. To his followers, the instigator of these acts was a man born to be remembered, a man of great intellect dedicating his life in the pursuit of pleasure.

On entering the entrance hall of the dominical now occupied by the granddaughter of the occultist and spiritualist famed for the previous wickedness, waiters wandered around handing out welcoming glasses of champagne to arriving guests as a Jethro Tull tribute band lodged in a balcony entertained them. Most of the guests quickly wandered off into side rooms to disrobe and adorn long hooded cloaks over their naked bodies. Others made final arrangements to their Pan costumes or other animalistic attire. There were Satanists, reincarnationists and your common garden witches mingling with groups of neo-pagans like themselves. There was no sign of any animosity or bigotry seen when different mainstream followers come together. The average age was slightly younger than that seen at an Anglican Church congregation, but still old and probably getting older. Nonetheless, one or two outstanding attractive young maids with strong Cornish and Dorset accents attracted the eye. He even recognised the face of a morning news presenter accompanied by her toyboy.

It was an occasion when anything could be said and taken to be true. As they waited and drank their champagne, Steve listened to an informative monologue from a nearby droll cross-dressing Satanist, porting a monocle expertly on his left eye, and dressed in an obviously custom made brightly coloured frilly French maid ensemble as there could not possibly be a standard off the shelf size for a fellow of his gigantic size. This *bon vivant* announced that perspicacity was a wonderful thing; edifying in many ways; and to understand evil, you had to experience it. It was enticing and very addictive. Heaven must just be full of dull leaden prigs as the only way not to be sinful was to do nothing and say no to anything risky. These poor souls would only be happy if every committed sin was visibly shackled to the offenders. This holier than thou brigade only existed to besmirch the activities of others. They forgot that their Church enjoyed a good carnival and no one knew more about zymurgy than them. Their vineyards and beehives once supplied the ingredients to make the wine and mead consumed at all major religious and secular events. Religious zealots were mad as a hare and would happily eliminate anyone not like them. Without earthy perversity, there could be no virtuosity. Man would never have left the treetops to create inventions that have made our abodes delightful places to live. Life was about diversity. Prostitutes and rent boys had to make a living as well while their presence helped alleviate the pressures placed on novice nuns and choirboys when priests failed to live up to their vows.

The main ritual part of the night started when the doors to the grand hall swung open and a wizard called the assembly to order. The high priestess wrapped in a golden robe and antler headgear waited with her inner circle on a makeshift stage, either side of them masked handlers held their birds of prey, as dancing flute and fiddle players led the brethren towards the altar. Choral chants accompanied the summons to join together to respect the past and to welcome the commencement of a new cycle in their calendar. These formalities went on until the clock struck midnight. Thereafter, doors swung open to allow trays of food and cauldrons of alcohol to appear amidst cries of encouragement to start the bacchanalia and to bring new life into the world. The young maidens looked suitably worried at this point. In the end, like any other decadent gathering, the event was just an excuse to get incredibly drunk, smoke dope and partake in tomfoolery.

Steve's own attempt at taxidermy would signal the end of this phase in the couple's lives. After several sessions of watching a skilled hand turn once loved pets into stuffed hallway features, Steve felt ready to embark on a stuffed animal composition for his required art project, which would form part of the annual college art show. The materials for the composition would be errant animals wandering about the neighbourhood. Mi-Cha wanted him to include a dog in his project, as the meat would allow her to make a large batch of bosintang. Despite the proposition that a plate of this soup would be better than Viagra, the idea was rejected. The likelihood of seizing a dog undetected was much lower than just enticing local cats with sprigs of catmint, supplied by a fellow Wiccan follower. Anyway, he was a dog lover at heart. His aim was to denote urban decay by having a clutter of cats eating clearly recognisable human faeces leaking from ripped plastic bags from well-known supermarkets. This piece of art would have been one-upmanship on Damien Hirst.

Unfortunately, things did not go to plan. Having to learn on the job, meant the depletion in the local cat population was higher than even Steve expected, as he had to discard many early attempts. Mi-Cha tried not to waste the meat by either boiling it to make a traditional Korean health tonic or casseroling it with plenty of thyme, which was purported to be how the Swiss ate cat meat. The thought of catching mad cow's disease by eating animals that ate meat never crossed their minds. In the end, there was just so much cat meat around that they soon got fed up with it. The proliferation in the disappearance of cats became quickly evident when the missing posters appeared all over the local lampposts and fencing. In the end, the neighbourhood became frenetic with worry about their pets as the early rumours of a wild beast on the loose and blaming curry and kebab takeaway shops proved unfounded. On one occasion, a local twitcher barely escaped with his life when cornered and accused of mass murder by a horde of irate pet lovers. It did not help his chances of survival when he robustly stated that cats massacred the urban wildlife.

Animal Rights activists got involved when carelessly disposed of remains appeared around the area. The dedication of these activists in hunting down abusers of animals was common knowledge. Pet owning residents willingly allowed them to organise surveillance at key points in the area. Their door-to-door investigations collated the dates of disappearances, which indicated a tsunami radiating outwards from the street the couple's rented flat resided. The need to finish his project on time forced Steve's hand and led to his downfall. Although the evidence against him would not hold up in court, his detected presence around the times of the last few abductions, alerted the protectors of the animal kingdom. This was all the Animal Rights activists required to advance their investigation. The military wing of the organisation then took over. This hooded well-armed heavy mob, which would scare the shit out of any hard man, paid the couple a late-night visit. Luckily for the miscreants, the reinforced locks of the main door to the flat delayed entry long enough to stop the activists from conducting life-threatening retribution before shouts warning of the arrival of the police caused them to withdraw. As a result, the activists only had enough time to find the nearly finished art exhibit, destroy it then inflict pain on the couple by cracking some ribs and splitting lips. Steve with Mi-Cha on toll decamped early next morning, abandoning their studies to head down the coast for a quieter spot to live.

PLEASURABLE GOINGS-ONS

Five minutes after leaving the flat for his midweek
evening soiree, Steve reaches the old town proper and
heads to the Queen Charlotte pub at the corner of
King George Street. It has been his habit for the last
year to visit this pub on the way to his regular
appointment with Julia. Her house is located on a
closed side street at the far end of this street on the
right-hand side. This is not the reason for choosing
this watering hole for a few drinks before partaking in
some congenial fun with Julia. He just likes to observe
the young while consuming his ale. It is also a good
spot for buying reliably good resin and cocaine. The
refurbished pub has fumigated itself of the
melancholic and the clock-watcher hugging their
pints, they are no longer welcomed. No one rants here
as people with strong views are dissuaded from
joining this trendy society. This pub is all about
attracting the right sort of consumer with space
compartmentalised to attract the comfortable young,
the self-confident who have the right cool attitude.
Lowly housing scheme dwellers would use direct
language in describing the behaviour of most drinkers

here, not nice euphemisms.

Fraternisation with the less endowed is not welcomed here. For those less fortunate, their acquired dispositions when growing up dictate whether they will go on to create a heaven or hell on earth. Most of them will not see the doors of opportunity easily opened. Many will never reach their full potential. Forever not letting go in adulthood to enjoy life to its full, remaining cocooned in protective wrapping, always suspicious of others. They live in fear that if they ever took the plunge they would never find a safety net to stop them falling or they fear coming to the conclusion that their acquired values are false when exposed to the cold light of experience.

The outside of the pub gives the false impression that the interior will be that of a small old fashion inn. It has a navy-blue façade with a small entrance door to one side and a long rectangular glass panelled window dominating the rest of the exterior. Below this window beer drop doors cover a chute for rolling kegs into the cellar. Thick black paint conserves the wooden beer drop doors, the main entrance and the window panels. The name of the pub adorned in gold lettering runs along the gap above the window and entrance. Thick bullseye glass windowpanes obscure the interior from prying eyes. Its hanging pub sign presents the face of a mixed-race woman wearing a colourful-feathered bonnet. In the early evening, the first person seen on entering the pub is usually old Bert, observing the world around him, as he sits at a table near the fireplace. He has been coming to this pub in all its manifestations for fifty years and is tolerated by the

bar staff and regulars. On face value, he is completely
out of place with the rest of the clientele. Nonetheless,
he is accepted, because of his timeless dry humour,
his intolerance to lickspittles of this world and the
fact that living a few doors down the street gives him
squatters' rights. Nothing matters to him nowadays
as he had long ago lost any emotional attachment to
anything. His redeeming feature is to resist the
temptation in old age to blight the happiness of
others.

On entering the pub, it looks narrow with a small bar
on one side and the aforementioned fireplace on the
other. However, beyond this scene, the pub broadens
to reveal an L shaped interior with a long gallery at
the back housing another bar and a small stage at its
far end. Air conditioning ensures a healthy supply of
air circulates the whole premises during peak
drinking hours. There is a bright modern feel to this
part of the pub. The décor here clearly states which
part of society is welcomed. The owner of the bar has
successfully established a social space to attract the
most demanding of cliques, the savvy and the
beautiful: the people who follow the right trends
before the masses copy them. Chic musical tastes,
clothes and physical looks differentiate them from the
herd. To the right of the stage emergency exit doors
open onto a lane and are used to let additional air into
the premises when the air conditioning fails in hot
barmy days. Regular amateur jazz and folk-rock
concerts along with pub quizzes and comedy hours
keep midweek drinkers entertained. There is even a
consecutive weekly speed dating night for the lonely of
each recognised sexual orientation: gay, lesbian,

transgender and heterosexual. At the weekend, the regulars entertain themselves with the help of a video jukebox. Despite the offer of good discounts from TV companies, the pub owner refuses to have sports channels relentlessly broadcasting away.

Private behaviour does not define a person, only in a social setting, can anyone be observed, judged and categorised. In nature, it is not necessarily the beautiful that win but it does help enormously in human society. The divinely perfect being seeks out others with the same destiny of living a pleasant rewarding life. Growing up these people encounter less alienation, gain confidence through higher self-esteem and are more likely to not develop serious anti-social habits. It is eugenics in action as the acceptable intermingle with the ultimate aim of improving the genetic quality of the human population, hoping to pass on their perceived superior human genetic traits. Social engineering achieved through sexual promiscuity rather than political manipulations. They come from various social strata; there are elitists, cash-rich liberals, friends with benefits enjoying all the earthly pleasures and beautiful libertines wishing to be seen. They believe that genetics have given them a natural superiority. Any harm is self-inflicted as they live in an age when the main desire is to live an exciting life without conscious thought of dying. They appear not to be touched by the perplexities that befall the less fortunate. However, the superiority paraded by their clothing and fashionable accessories cannot always hide what lies underneath. Prick their bubbles of pretence and they are revealed the same as everyone else.

Modern pitfalls effect all the young as exposure to the harsh realities of human behaviour comes sooner than with previous generations. In many cases, overexposure to extremes causes them to develop a hard skin, a selfish attitude, or cynical leanings at a younger age so consequently making these people resolute in their quest for self-gratification. An Italian once said the big difference between Europeans and the inhabitants of this country was net curtains. Now, no one under thirty has a private life anymore as everything about them is in the open. Promiscuous behaviour is public information. They would be lost if Wi-Fi stopped working. Social networking and life histories are available for all to see on the Internet. They know how to quickly record every moment of their lives but few know how that information is actually stored or how to completely erase it. Life revolves around fun with high-octane music and video used to drown out the cries of the suffering and to hide the faces of the piteous poor.

The bars here offer a fine collection of legalised concoctions: fortified wines, straw-coloured draught beer, bottled imported lager, tequila, rum and coke, and white spirit mixed with various fruit flavours satisfy the hedonistic consumers. Late in the evening, bombs, shots or shooters, strong cocktails loaded with caffeine, sugar and alcohol, provide immediate highs by suppressing the depressant effect of alcohol. It is absinthe and Viagra rolled into one for the young. Legal drug taking condoned as the immediate commercial and tax benefits outweigh the negative long-term effects. In addition, for those searching for a panacea to bless them with divine pleasure, happiness pills can be bought and kept in the pocket to invigorate the mind when required. Private transactions allow the exchange of various banned or disapproved substances promising such effect. Illegal recreational drugs produced in failed states around the world and legal chemical highs imported from China are always much sought after. The clientele vary from officer cadets from the nearby military training academy, middle-class anarchists, the idol and, of course, the addicts. Party drugs like Spice and K2 raise energy levels and lower inhibitions. Used on their own synthetic legal highs are deemed safe but can cause adverse effects when mixed with alcohol, creating psychotic symptoms similar to excessive dope use. The Chinese legally reaping revenge for the opium inflicted on them by the old British Empire. Synthetic legal drugs are preferred as they are harder to detect and easily acquired, whereas, supplies of hard drugs can be sporadic and unsafe. Police tolerate dope here, as they deem the clientele respectable and not likely to cause trouble. Despite the letter of the law, they have no wish to criminalise them. Drug taken is so ingrained in modern culture that it is perverse logic to allow only the criminal elements to make all the profit from its production and sale.

Steve speaks familiarly to old Bert and the bar staff when he enters the pub. Bar staff like regulars as it enhances the sense of security. While waiting for his dealer, Steve observes and listens to snapshots of conversation around him. He enjoys the naïve frankness of the discussions and the selfish motivations of the young. It is his aphrodisiac to put him in the mood. European au pairs congregate near the bar waiting to be pulled, making no attempt to whisper their conversations in the assumption that no one understands them, the common language of English only used when ordering drinks or stating the obvious. The local girls are equally indifferent when talking about sexual activity but the reasons for no decorum is more down to ignorance and the copying of behaviour seen in racy TV soap operas. One female expresses her disdain for her last sexual partner:

"It is fucking mental as he said his real name was Mark. Who cares if they are married or not, I always throw them out afterwards."

Her friend says fair play to her.

Officer cadets chat about the lack of secrecy of a fellow cadet about her sexuality. The posters around her bed and in lockers are a giveaway. Instead of male studs from the movies or the world of sport, she has female pop stars and firm limb scantily attired female tennis players.

A large powerful Aussie male in the company of two silly girls tells them to drink up as he wants to shower and they can help wash his back. A spoilt son complains that his parents bought him a flat without private parking. He then expands his grudge with talk about the old hoarding money, not for physical needs but for the psychological comfort that comes from ensuring they possess something worthwhile to make sure the family keeps in contact with them. With consumerism comes the responsibility to spend to keep the economy healthy and that lot are letting everyone down. If fifty percent of their money held in bank accounts disappeared overnight, they would not miss it. It could clear the national debt, but lucky for them we live in a multi-party state, otherwise, their excess money would be seized. Old people are miserable pricks anyway and take everything the wrong way even when you offer to help them in supermarkets or elsewhere. Money is not of much use to people over seventy, younger relatives should have their money before they go senile and have it conned from them. They do daft things when they get to old age. The grand uncle of a friend was a bachelor all his life then one day he married a woman half his age, rewrote his will leaving everything to her, cutting off his relatives, complete madness. You would think he would have wanted to leave behind something for his relatives. A son of the local MP recognises Steve when ordering drinks at the bar, suggests he should get himself into parliament, as that is where the big money resides. Steve reflects that this is the second person to make this suggestion. Mind you, he thought he could easily enough rant on about jobs and prosperity like the current local MP. The young man walks away explaining to his friends that he never sees his father as he is always up town while his mother spends all her time in the country attending her garden. The gardener is fucking her while his father is screwing his research assistant, a pretty girl who is keen to advance.

Steve is well aware that he is one of the oldest

regulars in the pub. In fact, it amazes him where the young around him go after they hit their mid-thirties. By all rights, if these people held the values they professed this place would attract many more people of similar age to him. They definitely must revert to type and become boring like their parents. The sexual adventures of the young cause Steve to reflect on his good fortune. In particular, Mi-Cha has unspoken forbearance for his wandering eye. Steve has had casual affairs with a number of women so his infatuation with the feminist Julia is not a surprise to her. Mi-Cha has no interest in adventurous eroticism so if Steve finds a willing collaborator to experiment with so what. Their liaison had developed into a business building enterprise rather than primarily motivated by her need for sex. She takes it for granted that after he has had his fill he will come back to her. She never shows any sign of resentment or protest. In western eyes, she is shy, withdrawn and subjugated. She on the other hand is resolute in the pursuit of material happiness and the acquisition of lovely things by working hard to obtain wealth, so long as it is literally free love and done outside the flat then she lets him have his fun. Her own vice is now online gambling which takes up her slack time when waiting for clients to contact her. From Steve's perspective, he naturally believes sexual liberation is good for women and men. Sexual morality should not be constrained by insane prohibitions, foolish intolerance and ruthless denial to all the possibilities imaginable. Julia has released a storm of physical passion with a strong desire for promiscuous behaviour that arouses him so guaranteeing his return for more. Julia does have curiosity about the part Mi-Cha plays in his life and has demanded answers to her questions. She is prone to unjustifiable jealousy due to irresistible subconscious impulses brought on by the late release of her excessive sexual cravings. Julia wants Steve to dedicate more time to her and fantasises about weekends away to conduct risky outdoor lovemaking. Foolish thoughts like escaping to the countryside to make love in a glade followed by skinny-dipping in the cool waters of a river. At the end of the day, Mi-Cha is too valuable a financial asset to give up and Julia just has to accept the situation. Life is perfect for Steve so why spoil it: rompish sexual activity with Julia and a well-ordered home with Mi-Cha. Once Julia's parents guessed the full extent of the tripartite relationship they attempted to break it up, without success as the more they remonstrated about the choice of her affections, the more Julia held steadfast to the arrangement. It would take a sweeping incident to shake Julia out of her compulsions and the unrealistic conviction that Steve would leave Mi-Cha for her.

Don Juan leaves the pub before it gets into full swing and heads to his señorita's residence. The house is down a mews consisting of pretty dwellings that once housed stables and small businesses. Julia's house and the ones joined to it are almost identical with the bottom floor dominated by a garage fronted with a pair of large swing doors. Adjacent to the garage doors is a long narrow vertical window frame to illuminate a stairway then the main entrance door followed by a standard size panelled window frame to let light into the front room. The second floor has three identically standard size window frames, one above the garage and the other two above the ground floor living space. The exterior walls and window frames are painted white while all the doors have a rich glossy black finish. When Steve lets himself in with the key provided to him the modern interior is revealed as a well-kept bright room with rugs on a wooden floor surrounded by walls painted in a pleasing light grey. A well-designed kitchen and small outside drying area are located at the back. A small recess between the kitchen and front room is used as office space. The interior has a similar layout to a modern terrace house with an open planned downstairs with three bedrooms, a box room and toilet upstairs. There is also access to a loft and cellar. The skirting, ceiling coves, interior window frames with intact wooden shutters are pristine white, while, the furniture is a mix of ebony and pine effect wood. In the front room, the grey of the large settee matches the colour of the walls. Most of the colour in the rooms comes from the patterns of the floor rugs and the rich grain of the varnished floors. Since the structure is obviously Georgian, it means the rooms are broader with higher ceilings. Georgian interiors render themselves for easy reconstruction to reflect modern tastes and requirements. This meant in most conservation areas, all that remained were the original external brick fabric of the buildings. Steve reflected that old Bert now might have the only dwelling in the area where the interior fittings are still genuine period pieces.

The noise of the shower indicates that Julia is upstairs preparing herself for him. To pass the time until she presents herself, Steve flicks through her mail and diary to see if any pressing business or council work may be causing her concern and consequently interfere with their bedroom exertions. Next, he briefly picks up and browses the cover of a novel that Julia is trying to find time to read: a modern classic about a self-obsessed hero unravelling a great mystery only to become disenchanted by its denouement. After discarding the paperback on the coffee table, Steve heads into the kitchen to take a bottle of white wine out of the fridge, uncorks it and places two glasses next to the resting bottle. Presently, Julia makes her appearance and smooches down on the settee facing Steve with her arms wrapped round her bent knees. The tang of minted breath due to just cleaned teeth temporarily overwhelms the scents from the applied body lotions. Underneath her white comfy bathroom robe is a matching combo of tight-fitting ruby red latex panties and crop top. Her blond hair has streaks of red tints that match her eyeliner, painted lips and ankle length socks. To finish the effect a pair of little devil horns adorns her head. Steve sits down next to her and asks how her day had gone. She smiles indicating with her shoulders that it was so-so. Getting up she lets the robe slip off her as she heads back up the steps. Steve gets the wine from the kitchen, takes the already prepared rollups from his discarded jacket, picks up the robe and follows her up to the bedroom. If alternative universes exist with a new one created for each different possible outcome of an event then a doppelganger somewhere is in for a horrible time tonight.

JULIA AND HER FAMILY

Six months before, Steve had made the excuse to Mi-Cha of having to go up town to a party central office local council policy review to escape with Julia to visit her parents in the Cotswolds. The arranged visit gave Steve the opportunity to assess the lay of the land. They had set out at dusk on an autumnal evening to arrive at their destination around ten, giving them enough time to say hello, have a drink then go to bed. On the way up, Steve daydreamed in the front passenger seat as Julia initially cut west across the country before turning back onto a fast road to take them up to Tewkesbury, an intact ancient town at the confluence of the Severn and the Avon. It was a town with a dark and brutal past. Now, its abbey was considered the best-conserved medieval parish church in the country because local nobles had stopped its ransack during the reign of Henry the Eighth by paying a sum sufficient to gratify this self-declared leader of its Church. The old town now resided within three main roads of black and white timbered houses, surrounded by a maze of small courts and narrow alleyways containing tiny cottages with lead framed windows. Colourful medieval banners hung from all the houses giving the place a festive air.

Julia had set herself up as a wellbeing consultant offering step-by-step guidance. Help started from something as practical as just reorganising a wardrobe to make choosing attire more relaxing; guidance on creating a more balanced nutritious diet; or de-cluttering an apartment to make it a tranquil living space. For people requiring a re-assessment of their lives, individual and family workshops were available to redirect or focus priorities; consultations to free your thinking potential to cope better in today' s hectic world or help in identifying and changing unhealthy patterns in daily life. She even had a range of wholesale bought products to sell to de-stress rooms and its occupants. All this would unblock trapped natural energy to turn leaden lives into golden ones. The biggest earnings derived from corporate work where stress management courses enabled executives and middle line managers to establish the right work to life balance to maximise productivity; effectively getting the workforce to toil harder, while at the same time create the illusion they had improved the use of their personal time, or what careerists called downtime.

Steve had finally possessed Julia one night in her townhouse after coming in to have a nightcap to unwind after a late council session. She was particularly wound up about an inane decision to leave council premises lighting on throughout the night for health and safety reasons, which insisted that night security staff had to be able to see what they were doing. The cost of the installation of individual switching in each corridor and office to allow guards to switch on and off lights as they went along would have been prohibitive; estimated to take fifteen years before savings on electricity usage would match the initial cost of upgrading the lighting system. Naturally, she thought they were missing the big picture in that the council should take the lead in encouraging commercial and private buildings to switch lighting off at night. As they sat down on the sofa Steve thought, it was now or never. For the last couple of months, he had been listening to her highly-strung laments and had enough. As he thought, when he knew her better he discovered that behind the perfect diction was an emotionally damaged person. He either had to make his move now or move on, something had to change.

Julia came from an old school family who saw their work as a duty and not a means of earning a living. With upbringing came responsibility and theirs was to be the guardians of the nation's culture, in other words, protect civilisation. Although classified as being part of the baby boomer generation that could enjoy life to the full without financial worries, their inherited decorum restrained everything they did, all based on old-fashioned morals to do the right thing for king and country. They were part of the front line that resisted any change to a privileged system based on heritage and loyalty to the crown. They saw themselves as rooted in the country's traditional values where everyone had their place in society. A time when the nation was populated with local shopkeepers and tradesmen ever ready to go up to the big house to offer their services. Being a good subject to them meant living life in a precise old-fashioned middle-class manner. This was no nostalgia for a bygone age. Their perceived rank in society gave them their pride and sense of self-worth. It also made them intuitively distrustful and nervous when the masses expressed any disquiet. To the vast majority of their fellow citizens they were living relics to a way of life that was extinct and incongruous.

Julia was a product of a marriage of convenience between two aging dedicated professionals, who both did not want a personal life to distract them from their work or hinder any possible advancement. The marriage prevented any adverse innuendos being associated with them. Their profession, in this case, was classical music performers. Her mother was a cellist and her father a lead violinist. The irony for Julia was the strings represented the soul of the orchestra allowing composers to express heartfelt emotions of which she saw precious little as a child. They never developed a strong urge to take an intimate interest in her or had any inclination to pressurize her to produce offspring of her own to continue the survival of their genes prior to their own demise. They were indifferent to the biological reasons for existing. No good or bad social interplay, just polite duty to ensure she had the best of education to allow her to quickly stand on her own feet. In recent times, when given the chance the cellist did make an effort to emit a sturdy-heart-felt rendering warmth while the violinist maintained a plaintive resolute persona.

Marrying or remarrying within the same field allowed professional people to gain a partner that was familiar to the expected demands placed upon a relationship by the chosen profession. Military personnel, doctors and politicians all find the need to couple up with people within their own sphere. People from the same profession also tend to have similar lookouts and values. For many changing partners within the same background just meant replacing the body, as attitudes and values remained the same. To outsiders, they all just appeared to look and behave the same.

The child was an unintentional consequence of initially sharing a bed together; an inconvenience not repeated by a mutual agreement to have separate bedrooms. Their work schedule required a lot of travelling and time apart so the last thing they wanted was a child. Being the lead violinist meant that her father was the most important person after the conductor of the orchestra. He played the solo if no guest violinist was present and ensured the tuning of all instruments prior to the impresario arriving on stage. He had to be able to continually observe the conductor to pick up instructions for the rest of the violin section to follow. Her mother played in the cello section of the orchestra. At various periods in their lives, they had worked for the BBC Concert Orchestra, National Orchestra of Wales and Birmingham Philharmonic Orchestra. They also performed chamber concert music at various festivals around the world.

Julia's political pursuit had made her just as selfish and egocentric as any accused male political counterpart, and in many ways aped her parent's behaviour. By necessity, she adopted the method and the rhetoric of the established order, and her strategy for success was to be more politically motivated and active than that of her opponents. No matter how noble the cause, activists can build up a chip on their shoulder or become myopic. Unfortunately for some dysfunctional souls, life had a way of intervening to upset the apple cart. In this case, feminism and environmentalism alone could not replace a need for emotional comfort; it only filled the void with dogma and purpose for continuing but did nothing to resolve the problem of an unsettled heart and the effect this had on the subconscious. Her single-mindedness had roots leading back to her childhood. She had learnt from an early age to stop the mind dwelling on negative thoughts by studying hard. Keeping the mind busy only suppressed unhappy memories, unpleasant feelings and regrets, preventing reflection to bring peace of mind and resolution of past emotional conflicts or traumas.

As a wellbeing consultant, she knew that relationships were important; a kiss was the symbolic sharing of the spirit, as one's breath united with the other's, two becoming one. Instead of looking for a relationship for shelter, to fulfil physical or financial needs, true companionship worked as a catalyst to accelerate spiritual awakening to release your being to point it in a direction where it could grow. Rapid personal development was only possible when both parties functioned as foils and mirrors for each other. In essence, love shifted a person away from egotism to a shared existence, a self-giving existence that raised consciousness, as each partner became the check and balance to help protect the body to enrich the soul by providing physical relaxation and spiritual completeness: carrying each other's burden to share angst and help lessen any pain. If one of the participants remained egoistic, then the relationship remained forever flawed, continuing life together only satisfied materialistic or worse still psychotic needs. Nevertheless, like many experts, Julia never applied advice to herself. She had brief affairs due to peer pressure to engage in sex but never opened up her heart in fear of rejection. Instead, she played the role of the happy unconcerned about life beautiful person. In her daily life, she quietly dreaded that emotional outbursts would devalue her and lay bare psychotic tendencies, which would exclude her from participating in political life. She carried the sins of parents who showed no love or gave her no sense of belonging. She lived her life as a stranger waiting for an invitation to join the party.

Steve, after putting his empty glass on the coffee table, pulled Julia towards him and wedged his lips to her mouth. Throughout the next five or so minutes, his lips held steadfast to her mouth as he rose up her dress, stripped the tights and pants off her and tore off her top and bra to reveal her breasts, all the time groping her to get her into a position to make it easy for him to penetrate. Hearts pounded, air gusted and gulped from lungs as Julia's breasts shook under Steve's indecorous assault. Quite simply he manhandled her while unzipping his trousers into a position where her legs were pinned over his shoulders and her head banged against the lower back of the sofa. He overpowered her and drove on until he ran out of juice.

All his frustration released for having to spend all evening listening to a silly debate instead of sitting in a warm pub enjoying a few pints of ale. Traumatised, Julia, after initially attempting to bite and scratch for all her worth, remembered a lecture once given by a feminist group to offer passive resistance and to play dead. It may have also just been the instinctive response of an animal in accepting its fate when overpowered by superior predators. Regardless of the true reason, all the way through her silent protest, Steve remained completely oblivious to this defiant act.

Afterwards, they briefly held their positions with eyes transfixed on each other until she managed to rock him off her with his unhindered consent. They remained next to each other as he called a spade a spade and preached his love for her. He could not have had gone on without having her. If he had not made a move he would have ended up like Simon and no way that was going to happen. He was an emotional man without her education and self-control but all the same a human being who wanted love. She was the most perfect woman he had ever met and he would never give up on her. He looked remorseful and full of guilt for his shoddy act of seduction. Pouring another drink, he settled in for a couple of hours of persuasion mixed with remorse for his action. Quiet talk filled with long pauses followed:

"Forgive me"

"I hate myself"

"I will always be sorry"

"I have been burning with fever, night and day, for months"

"I just cannot get you out of my mind"

Like a good angler who changed his fly and tackle to catch his prize, he tried various lines to cajole a response from her.

"I am not trying to make excuses"

"You know we like each other"

"You send me crazy"

"As long as I am able to do so, you can count on me"

"I urge you to give me a chance"

During this spell, Julia cuddled up in a ball, was pinned against the side the sofa, and wrapped in what remained of her clothing. Although not convinced, confusions troubled her as no man had ever told her he loved her in such a heartfelt way. In the past, declared love was the expected expression of play rather than the pure outburst of violent unexpected passion. She knew that Steve fancied her and she also knew there was a grain of truth in the proposition that sex had previously crossed her mind, but she never thought that he would pounce on her. Finally, feelings of fatigue and continued bewildered ended this tête à tête and they both went their separate ways.

Next time they met, Julia simply left her front door
open allowing the hesitant Steve to decide whether he
should enter or not. They awkwardly sat next to each
other on the same sofa as the night before.

'Well?'

After several moments, they hugged. He promised to
be her counsel and friend. For the following next few
months, Steve was the perfect companion for Julia
and passed every test put in front of him. The sores
after their first full contact could not allow her to
forget that it was rape but being able to express anger
and frustration at another human being had made her
feel real. She convinced herself for the first time that
she knew what normal relationships were like. Life
was not perfect and had to be lived. Everyone had
emotional baggage and from time to time used each
other as punching bags.

Childhood for Julia was one of periodic upheaval from
one abode to another. After her birth, she lived with
her parents until breast feed then she was passed
between grandparents to allow her mother to
recommence her career after respectfully observing
the correct period of confinement. Each of her
grandparents passed her about until their natural
deaths forced her parents to send her to boarding
school. During this period, she never experienced any
early friendships with children of her own age. There
was never the necessary experience of rough and
tumble play to gain skills or to acquire good
instinctive responses to enable healthy participation
in adult social activities. Instead, her early memories

were filled with sitting quietly in large smoke-filled
cold draft ridden rooms listening to clocks ticking as
her guardians silently read. She remembered a little
dog that used to growl and snap at her, a nasty little
thing loved by one of her grandparents. It was a frosty
adult world with no humour or energetic ways to
release tension. At boarding school, she remained the
youngest in her year throughout her childhood due to
the initial necessity of her parents to unload her into
the hands of others when her grandparents died. She
tended to miss out on camaraderie so withdrew into
herself: the conversations of older girls generally
excluded her from the rest of the form; her smaller
physique was a handicap on the playing fields. Sports
never became her forte.

Although her parents were time mean they spared no
expense to give her the best education possible. The
boarding school was for privileged children. It
provided children with everything required to become
an established member of the privileged class. It even
had a debating chamber to prepare the chosen for
future political or public service posts. It was an
establishment where emotions were drilled out of you,
although in her case they were just buried deep
within her. Debating skills, one-to-one tuition and
elocution lessons gave her a rich vocabulary and the
right accent to succeed. Talking well gave her an
outward maturity that hid infantilism. Her music
lessons included the piano, and from an early age, she
practised the instrument so deftly played by her
mother. Lugging her cello around continually brought
to mind her abandonment by her parents. In years to
come just seeing a cello brought back all her bad

childhood memories. She also had an angelic voice that meant conscription into the school choir, a choir specialising in renaissance chanting performed in the school's private chapel. Outside life was limited; she was only guaranteed to meet her parents on Christmas day and during the scheduled annual summer break. Otherwise, she usually spent the holiday periods at the boarding school with other abandoned children, when matters for the State or high business engaged those children's parents. Sometimes she spent a part of the vacations at the home of a fellow pupil, brought home to share companionship and domestic intimacy with strangers. Naturally, resentment and loathing of her parents boiled within her especially when returning pupils competed to express their excitement, adventures and gifts betrothed on them by loving parents. From an early age, she felt abandoned and believed that she had to stand-alone in this world. The barriers set up for self-protection were those of an immature vulnerable child not a world wise pragmatic adult. They were barriers that were unbending, unsophisticated and easily broken. All the way through her life, she held back her true emotions, warmth and capacity to love. She trusted no one believing that the lack of warmth shown by her own family was somehow her fault. Within her, there was a hunger for an overwhelming love response from another human being, fed by deep unhappiness and torment.

Financially she would never have any concerns for the rest of her life. Inheritances from both sides of the family would eventually come to her. At an early age, the Georgian townhouse in Hayes-by-the-Sea became available to her as a retreat from studies at Cambridge. Following school tradition, she chose an all-girls college to ensure no distractions prevented her from obtaining the accreditations required for fast-track success, a tradition that went back to the days when Cambridge only formally accepted female students from approved private Church of England schools. Here, Julia's interest in politics blossomed. Her upbringing suggested a career in the political right but her interest in feminist issues ultimately dissuaded her from joining a male-dominated party. Instead, the attraction of the emerging environmental groups galvanised her, which although just as dictatorial in their beliefs on how the earth should be saved, they were sincere and as yet not stuck in a mire of self-interest greed or historic corruption scandals.

A sudden braking of the car woke Steve up as Julia recomposed herself after a fallow deer nearly ran into the front of the car. Luckily, no one was close behind them. This was the official welcome to the Cotswolds once famed for sheep and wool and whose landscape was immortalised by the music of Elgar. The brick of the southern counties left behind to be replaced by medieval cut stone. The idolised countryside of southerners with steeples touring above copses, hedge roads separating villages dressed in pleasing pale yellow Cotswold stone, and farms set in low undulating hills. To relax her Steve rubbed the top of her thighs leaving an index finger pressed into her as she changed gears to restart the engine. The journey continued without further hassle. The dark shallows of the distant hills contrasted sharply with the flatness of the valleys. Nowhere was there any hint that the Avon would join the longest tidal river in the country. It was only when they entered Tewkesbury by a low stone-built bridge crossing a floodplain down below the old abbey did they came upon the illustrious Shakespearean river. At that time of night, they could only sense the expanse of the floodplain rather than see it by the depth of the surrounding darkness as no artificial light shone there. In these fields, the Lancastrians laid dead after being massacred or chased into the abbey to be subsequently butchered. A bend on the road brought them into sight of the outskirts of the town with the illuminated tower of the abbey hailing them on the right-hand side of the road.

Prior to driving to her parent's house, Steve insisted on stopping at an alehouse for a drink under the pretext to allow his lover to relax and prepare herself for the next couple of days ahead of them. In truth, he wanted a drink and a smoke to get the stiffness out of his body as he presumed that the next couple of hours would be a formal banal affair. They stopped at the Royal Hop Pole hotel where Dickens reported that Pickwick drunk many bottles of port. The hotel rested on Church Street, the main thoroughfare. Its use as an inn went back three hundred years. A pub chain catering to the demands of the modern drinker had recently renovated it. There was now a long comfortable lounge split into adult only and family dining areas. The bar running parallel to the sitting areas had many types of local ale to tempt the traveller. A long narrow boxed-in garden, which once was part of the yard that horse drawn coaches would have pulled into ran down to the Severn, which at the time of their visit was as peaceful and calm as a well-maintained canal, due to the lack of any persistent rain.

The house of the parents was only a further couple of minutes drive up river from the hotel. The Edwardian built structure had not been renovated to cater for the demands of modern living; a single floor structure with its original features, no dormer loft conversion or any other modern protrusion. It backed onto the river on the same side as the pub but with better open views of the distant Malvern Hills behind it. They had moved there a couple of years ago when both of them gave up work. It was a three-bedroom house with separate reception, sun and dining rooms. The main rooms had large Persian carpets on top of parquet flooring. The hall and kitchen had decorative and rustic floor tiling respectively. Each bedroom had on-suite faculties. The kitchen and living room both had French windows that opened onto a protected stone patio and a lawn garden with a gravel path that ran all the way down to a fence, stopping at a gate that allowed access to the riverbank. In the mornings, soft sunlight lit the hills perfectly, and from the late afternoons, the back of the house became a suntrap.

The dining room was preserved for formal use as a dining area. A mahogany dining suite dominated the room. The table underneath a crystal candelabrum could comfortably seat six diners. On one wall, a display of matching framed pictures showed the couple performing with various orchestras over the lifetime of their careers. They rarely appeared together. Against another wall was a large matching mahogany bookcase, which gave a strong indication of the taste of the owners. Apart from the expected biographical and critical reviews of various composers and their works, the bookcase contained the complete hardback editions of Charles Dickens, Anthony Powell 's A Dance to the Music of Time compendium, novels by George Elliot, John Buchan, Thomas Hardy, Nevil Shute and other English fiction writers along with the works of historians A.J.P. Taylor and Max Hastings. The nearest example of modern fiction was a book by the unreadable Howard Jacobson. The cuckoo in the nest was an illustrated hardback edition to everyday knitting. A mahogany sideboard, exhibiting fine china serving plates and dishes, occupied the remaining window free wall.

The living room looked as if it should be a comfortable space to provide relaxation. The Town and House magazine could easily have done a feature on this living space. Although they preferred elegant Georgian pieces to the later heavier and darker Victorian and Edwardian period items, the furniture was an eclectic mix of pieces mainly inherited from relatives and some items bought from antique auctions. The latter being the Georgian pieces and the former the later period pieces. On the walls, oil landscapes and still life paintings, along with watercolours of local artists ensured that any visitor would not forget where he or she was. The principal colour of the floor length pleated curtains across the French windows matched that of the frames of the paintings. Two large matching sofas adorned with soft cushions dominated the space in the centre of the room. However, everything was too clean and formal, which denied the creation of a cosy feel demanded for real comfort. It simply did not look lived in and a guest would always feel conscious about dropping crumbs or spilling tea. There was no impression of warmth found in a loving home or signs of disorganisation to suggest any spontaneous relaxed act.

An expensive all-surround music system did suggest a love for music but examination of the cd collection indicated a restricted taste. There was no divergence or disturbance from a narrow spectrum, no mosaic to imply a varied, well-experienced life, only classical music and theatrical musical collections. No blues, jazz, folk or the dreaded popular music invaded this space. In their lifetime, nothing penetrated their orthodox appreciation of music. Swing meant nothing to them. The magic of Old Blue Eyes or Nat King Cole passed them by. The folk and rock eras left them cold. There was no place for the wallowing Bob Dylan, the pernickety Neil Young or the ostentatious Pink Floyd. Late seventies punk must really have seemed to them to be anarchy in the UK, and not expressed anger at the manipulation of music by big record companies. House music would have been equivalent to waterboarding and grunge was something the maid was told to clean out of the back from the oven. Even the power ballad era with full orchestral support did not manage to break through their barriers. No soft female vocals to suggest they once possessed a tender heart. If they ever had their song it probably was a Strauss Viennese waltz.

They never deviated from their chosen path, believing in all honesty that their taste was the envy of the world, followers of centuries of tradition, and never seeking to be trendsetters or rebels. Overall, nothing in the room gave any suggestion of the personality of the occupants it only reflected their status. The presence of her mother's cello within its mounted open case gave a hint of their profession. It could have been construed that this space was an elaborate burial chamber for this fallen and well-loved faithful friend. Her father's violin resided with other family valuables in a safety deposit box at the bank. A touch of arthritis in his right hand now spoilt any pleasure in handling the instrument. A piano in the sunroom sufficed for days when there was an urge to play music.

Julia's parents, Albert and Elizabeth both stood on the porch when they drove into the driveway. Quick handshakes and a kiss on the cheek expressed a polite welcome. The age difference between the parents was similar to that between Julia and Steve. Steve immediately noted that Julia had the same facial features as her mother but not her heavier bone structure. Maybe, being a late child by ageing parents meant the birth of a bit of a runt. After promptly placing their cases in the spare bedroom, they resumed their introductions in the living room. Both parents looked and acted like frosty academics that never got their hands dirty, with a dress sense that was old-fashioned even for their peers. They seemed awkward in the presence of a commoner like Steve. Her father had a pale complexion over a skeletal face with thinning grey sandy hair combed back behind rather large ears. His nose was hawkish and matched a strong protruding chin. By habit, he wore a checkered shirt with a plain tie, cardigan and jacket. He could easily be mistaken for a parish vicar. The hesitant handshake revealed long emaciated fingers to match his face. Her mother wore woollens in the form of a polo neck jumper and a thick long skirt. A little gold brooch with small diamond inlays was fastened to the jumper just above her heart. She was smaller and broader than her husband with a rosier complexion due to running around all day mollycoddling her husband. Her hair looked dyed. As expected, they spoke perfect English. Julia seemed awkward as well but for different reasons. The family history and the formal mannerism made it difficult for her to relax or jump into an off-the-cuff conversation. Like strangers, they talked about the weather and the journey up from the coast.

Steve eyed the furniture as he drank his coffee and wondered how he would survive two days here. He remained silent as the conversation centred on distant older childless relatives that their parents had been cultivating over the last couple of years. Her parents desired to be attorneys to their estates and have probate when these relatives died. Julia thought it was a macabre way to spend their retirement, while her parents believed that it was sensible to try to keep assets within the family. On listening to this familial chatter, Steve realised the financial worth of Julia's family; Julia was going to be very rich one day, richer than he first thought. A quick look across at her mother then dampened his interest as he estimated that the old dear had at least another twenty years in her. The probate ambitions did not always go to plan. One of the older relatives had recently upset her mother by physically forcing her off his property when he understood the intention of her unexpected and uninvited visit. Relative or not, no complete stranger was getting anything when he died, it made more sense to leave everything to a cats' home than see it wasted by her progeny. This propensity on seeking probates irritated Julia immensely and fuelled her rebellion against her class and to seek a more just and equal society.

As far as their own deaths were concerned both parents had the same unspoken desire. For different reasons, they wanted the husband to be the first to meet his maker. He did not want the inconvenience of running the house or ending up in an old folk's home. He was essentially sedentary, isolated from the rest of the world and completely dependent on his more active wife for his entire daily needs. Sometimes by accident, he would meet a neighbour and was obliged to have a brief chat but mostly he was like a household pet waiting at home. On the other hand, the mother honestly believed that his death would give her a new release of life. She could be out every day, spend more time stopping to chat with neighbours to find out the latest gossip; give some midweek time to a local charity shop; and enjoy shopping for groceries and preparing food that she liked. She knew that the local women's institute was a thriving and dynamic organisation with widows forever going on trips around the country and mainland Europe.

The soiree ended around midnight when they headed to their bedrooms. Tomorrow was going to be a busy day as they planned to show them the abbey then whisk them off to Gloucester to attend the Elgar recital festival at the Cathedral. The evening recital that day had the Cello Concerto in E Minor on the programme. The plan for Sunday was to return to the coast after a leisurely morning and early lunch.

Politeness summed up Saturday perfectly. They woke up, washed and dressed, sat down to breakfast, and then strolled into town along the riverbank to the abbey. On the way, Julia's feminist activities at college were the major topic of conversation. Apparently, a great aunt on her mother's side was a suffragette so female rebellion ran in the family. Julia pointed out that feminism had moved a long way since those days when it was all about the right of white middle-class women to vote. Life was pluralistic. Today, it was about the fight for free expression and the choice to do whatever you wanted. It was a bottom-up approach rather than behaving like stereotypes encouraged by academic white women. Modern feminists did not all have to agree about the same thing. Power politics enabled the pursuit of the interests of all women. It promoted aspirations, defying lazy stereotyping of genders, and stopping de-marginalisation. There were different types of feminist groupings ranging from political, poststructuralists to black and postcolonial feminism. The environment, abuse within the home, and the exploitation of women all round the world probably interested them more than anything else did. Women wanted to be individualists just like men. Economic gender equality with the same remuneration packages would advance that goal. As they reached the turn off that appeared on the left to Church Street, the conversation ended with Steve saying he liked the fact that the country was now full of female joggers. Everyone except Julia smiled at this concluding comment.

The view at the main gated entrance, showing the corner aspect of the abbey encompassing a large yew tree and large raised sarcophagi, was picturesque. Julia's father proceeded to divulge his local knowledge mixed with well-documented history of the abbey. He particularly noted that choral evensong service here was enchanting, and it was a pity to have to miss it. The bells summoning the parish to sit in the candle lit stalls to absorb the angelic late baroque sounds of Gibbons, Tallis and Byrd induced spiritual renewal. Like most churches in the country, the Normans founded Tewkesbury abbey in the twelfth century. In this case, due to the site's closeness to a ford that allowed safe crossing of the rivers. The magnificent tower and large arched western front contained local limestone. The high bevelled archway of the western front consisted of many tiered arches extending from the ground going right round the vault. Its uniqueness was striking. Inside, the light from the greatest example of original late medieval stain glass windows in the country made the interior feel intimate and warm. The undamaged heraldic floor tiles showed no ill effects from the Dissolution or traces of splatted bloodstains from the carnage of the War of the Roses. The butchered young prince lay entombed amid this medieval splendour. The

Lancastrian heir to the throne, Edward Prince of
Wales, and many prominent Lancastrian nobles died
during the battle or were brutally dragged from the
sanctuary of the church to be immediately
slaughtered. Next door, the restored presbytery
provided the town with a modern civic arts centre and
a comfortable place for tourists to have a deserved
break. Immediately across the road was a rival
tearoom within a thatched cottage. This gave the
party a choice of venues for a late morning cup of tea.

After several minutes of debate, the decision went in
favour of the thatched cottage for its historic
authenticity. The authentic looking pub further up
the street would have suited Steve more. In the
tearoom, the retired violinist expressed his well-
rehearsed views on orchestral music when Steve
asked him about his work. Classical music was
powerful, beautiful, moving, and elusive in a way no
other art form could convey. Although music itself had
no meaning, it helped individuals to reflect on the
inexpressible while it also engendered spiritual
fulfilment. An armoury of volume, rests, pedal point,
repeats and tremolo allowed transference of mood to
the listener. Orchestral music combined purity of form
with expression of emotion to create beauty.
Orchestral music allowed composers to create inner
lines of counterpoint, harmony and variation using
different sets of instruments. They composed a
tableau in colour whereas composers for soloists or
chamber ensembles worked in black and white. The
pedantic mannerism of Julia's father confirmed to
Steve that he was a bit of a pompous arse while her
mother was dismissed as a batty old fool, both

harmless but worth avoiding if pleasure was the name of the game. Years of being in the background made one of them quietly depressed and the other convinced to be an authority on all things to do with culture. When they ventured out into the real world they probably found the habits of their fellow citizens quaint and amusing, with no real comprehension on how others actually lived.

A stroll back to the house ended the first instalment of the entertainment. They agreed to be ready to leave for Gloucester at four in the afternoon. They would eat something in town then head for the Cathedral to be in good time to survey the architecture before taking their seats. That left the younger couple time on their own which they decided to use by sitting out in the back patio to enjoy the vista as Steve had a smoke. The older couple potted about doing normal Saturday afternoon activities. Her father merely retired to his desk, turned on the radio and spotlight, sat in his favourite hardback chair to listen to Radio 3 with the Mail newspaper spread out in front of him, as his wife tidied up around him moaning about his feet getting in the way. For Steve and Julia, it was the first time they ever spent a free weekend afternoon together. They were fish out of water. On Saturday afternoons, Steve was usually in the process of merrily getting smashed. Julia would normally be sorting out her correspondence and preparing her next week's schedule while listening to an audiobook. To obtain a quick quiet moment for himself, Steve headed down to the riverbank. Using the pretext to find out what fish a local angler was hoping to catch, Steve made use of his temporary escape to check his

phone for messages. He wandered back to the patio
when called. Late afternoon tea had arrived in the
shape of Julia's mother bringing out a tray on which
contained a pretty art decor tea service with a
selection of goodies from a hamper regularly ordered
from an up town store. The exhaled breath of her
mother indicated she enjoyed a discrete tipple when
alone in the kitchen. By way of a backhand
compliment, Steve suggested that she should open a
tearoom here. The young couple were told not to rush,
as the departure time was just to give her husband a
head start to get ready as he always took ages to get
out of the house. Slow to get out of the house, quick to
get back in.

Gloucester was still busy with shoppers when they
arrived in the car park just off the bus terminus. A
sixties type structure overlooking a maze of bus stops
that buses navigated by following a tricky one-way
system, as passengers perilously cut across bus lanes
to naturally get to their pickup spot as quickly as
possible. After a couple of sharp turns on foot, the
group reached Northgate reasonably quickly. This
wide pedestrian precinct street made it an ideal spot
to hold farmer and artisan markets. Rows of stalls,
selling everything from raw cuts of meat to scented
candles, on each side of the street stationed by
trueborn and as yet not banished Englishmen and
women. The bustling crowd augmented by groups of
Japanese and Chinese tourists, and boisterous
German, Italian and French youngsters on their first
school trip abroad; all their historic grievances
forgotten, as they mingled around the stalls after an
awe-inspiring visit to one of the best cathedrals in the

world. Gloucester like Lincoln was once a wool town; rivals that competed to be the capital of the wool industry in medieval Europe. Both towns had magnificent intact cathedrals with grand cloisters. Each diocese possessed a scribed copy of the Magna Carta. However, in the end both powerhouses fell when finance became the main driving force in commerce.

Their destination was the New Inn hotel, a grade one listed Elizabethan closed courtyard inn with intact original galleries, quite simply the best example of its kind. It was now a grille and carvery with reportedly six bars. This wetted Steve's appetite. He proposed they had a drink first before deciding on what to eat. To honour the festival Steve ordered a pint of Pomp and Circumstance ale while the rest shared a bottle of white wine. The courtyard was set out for a performance of an abridged version of Julius Caesar. A forty-minute play containing all the keynote speeches to allow the audience to understand that Brutus was a man of principle that put freedom and democracy above friendship while Mark Antony was an opportunist seizing the day. Because they were diners, they did not have to pay an entrance fee to watch Caesar being hacked to death on the senate steps. The backdrop of spectators crammed into the yard and on two floors of steep and tight gallery space raised the performance of the amateur actors, in essence enacting the same play that Shakespeare himself would have directed here over four hundred years ago. When it was time to eat Steve helped himself to all the cuts of meat on offer as the rest of the group carefully and gingerly selected small white meat cuts with a salad side dish.

They reached the Cathedral indirectly by opting to go
further up the Northgate to turn left into an old
monks' walkway that took them to the eastern side of
the Cathedral instead of walking straight down
Westgate to the main south porch entrance. This
allowed viewing of the whole exterior of the building
when the visitors walked in the grounds round to the
main entrance; a Romanesque archway with apostles
posted along the top looking sternly down which
imposed a feeling of holy meekness on anyone that
entered. The recital was to be played in front of the
high altar at the east window erected to commemorate
battles won in the Hundred Years War at Crecy and
Calais, seventy-eight by thirty-eight feet of stain glass
depicting feudal hierarchy from earth to heaven.
Nobles then bishops, kings, saints and disciples all
the way up to Christ and the Virgin Mary, finally to
God surrounded by angels praising him.

They reached their seats by a detour along the south
transept where resided the alabaster tomb of Edward
the Second so brutally departed from this earth for
having human frailties and more importantly for
losing his barons land and riches. The festival
programme notes indicated a mix of Anglican choral
music along with the Cello Concerto itself. Opening
with the choir singing O Hearken Thou, give unto the
Lord and Agnus Dei; followed by the concerto; and
finishing with Great is the Lord. The soulful mood of
the psalms and concerto suggested that a melancholic
evening lay ahead. No significant break was indicated
which given the surroundings would be difficult to

accomplish. In all, the timings of each piece indicated a total duration of around seventy minutes. The irony that a national radio broadcaster was transmitting the recital in its entirety live to the nation was not lost on Steve. He saw no additional benefit obtained by sitting in a freezing church. When the recital began, he spent most of his time waiting to tick off each piece, trying not to cough during quiet sequences, and, as instructed by the radio host, to applaud as loudly as possible to create the impression that the people at home were missing a once in a lifetime event. His discomfort was magnified by the combined effect of the surrounding cold air and the consumed beer had on his bladder. By comparison, most of the audience did give the impression of genuine enjoyment. It was an audience well versed in the music of Elgar that loved live performances. Their experience of such events amply displayed by the rugs wrapped rounds their legs and knees. An audience incredibly identical to each other, who lived in similar residences, which tonight probably lay empty for any enterprising burglar anticipating the movements of these well-to-do retirees.

In the car back to Tewkesbury Julia's mother explained that the concerto was written just after the First World War and reflected the despondency felt by the nation while Elgar himself was exhausted and depressed. For Steve, knowing the background to the score did not create a better appreciation of the work only astonishment they would deliberately want to spend a Saturday night inflicted with so much sorrow. She went on to volunteer her preference for Dvořák's Cello Concerto in B minor to Elgar's great work. In her mind, Dvořák was romantic music's most creative wizard. His concerto was a Mecca for cellists because it gave them recognition as virtuosi. No other cello concerto touched it in terms of size, expressive depth, melodic richness and formal perfection. The scoring required a full romantic orchestra and great technical ability. It inspired Elgar and others to write their own pieces. Musical historians quoted Brahms as being jealous when he first heard it. Although the highbrow critics in this country once branded Dvořák as a second-rate composer, his international appeal and popularity had never waned. The work was part of his successful American period and drew inspiration from black spirituals and American popular songs while still anchored in the Slavic tradition. All this diversity and blending of non-Anglo-Saxon sounds was probably the real reason why the highbrows here once dismissed it. Elgar and Dvořák were like chalk and cheese, one restraining passion and the other ebullient to show it.

Back in the house, it was still early for the younger couple when the older pair expressed a desire to unwind in their bedrooms prior to sleeping. This left Steve and Julia alone in the living room on the promise that they kept the sound down on the television. A bottle of wine meant for lunch on Sunday was ceremoniously given to them. As Julia poured the wine, Steve relaxed and thought quietly for a moment. He then got up and made a close inspection of the encased cello, which indicated that flexible clips held it in place. He duly unfastened the instrument free and pretended to Julia that he played it. Julia held her hands to her mouth trying not to giggle or spit out wine. This virtuoso thought it was time for a useful application for this torturous instrument. He laid it on the floor between the twin sofas and beckoned Julia to him. Whispered in her ear to put on that cd of the recording her mother was enthusiastic about then come straight back to him. He proceeded to undress her as she pretended astonishment at this indecent proposal. He stripped her slowly from top to bottom, kissing each new exposed part of flesh. He got down on his knees as he removed her trousers and silk panties. With his hands on her buttocks, he pulled her into his searching tongue. When satisfied that there was sufficient lubrication he theatrically danced round the cello and Julia, peeling off his clothes one article at a time in tune with the accompanying melody. Julia giggled while her eyes flashed between the prankster and the living room door. Steve then invited Julia to position herself between him and the cello to allow them all to join in the virtuoso performance of Catherine du Pre coming over the speakers. With her legs parted and backside raised, Steve gave the best performance he could muster to match the allegro of the first movement, nevertheless, as he was no spring chicken it pleased him to be able to conclude his contribution during the adagio section of the second movement. From now on, the sight of a cello would never bring feelings of foreboding to Julia ever again.

At breakfast, as her mother busied herself serving tea and cooked food she expressed delight at hearing them play her cd recording of Dvořák. She could not think of a better way to serenade her to sleep. Her husband thought she was getting battier as it sounded as if the tuning was off and all he heard was the sound of two cats scuffling. Haydn and Mozart symphonies with their quiet purity and repeated melodies were the best way to clear the mind late at night. Just try listening to one of Mozart's piano concertos. Steve pointed out that he liked the cut and thrust of the romantics, freely passing on his limited understanding of form by saying that he had caught a discussion on radio about musical scoring, which said all styles of Western music from classical, jazz to pop made excessive use of the 2-5-1 chord progression and limitless variations of it. The tonal scales of Western music rendered this progression pleasing to the ear. It was just the tempo and interplay between instruments that defined the styles. The stare from the old man's eyes easily indicated that he thought that Steve was an imbecile.

Sunday morning saw a similar schedule repeated except this time a quick car ride took them to Worcester to see its Cathedral. A Cathedral famed and rebuilt to house the body of the Magna Carta King in the centre of its chancel. A king so loathed by the nobles that they even considered replacing his family's dynasty by inviting the French to take over. It was once the diocese for the region but a resentful Henry the Eighth moved it to Gloucester because Worcester became a place of pilgrimage to see the tomb of his beloved elder brother, Arthur, once predicted to be a future renaissance king the country wanted. To further deter pilgrims the church, and in particular, the prince's tomb suffered desecration during the Dissolution. On arriving, they found that

Sunday worship prevented a tour of the vast interior
so to make up for this disappointment; Julia's father
trotted them across the road to see a statue of Elgar.
This cheered up Steve, as it was obvious that their
guide had not foreseen the aftereffects of a busy
Saturday night in a market town that attracted the
young from all across the region. Half-drunk beer
bottles, takeaway containers and condoms
decoratively bestrew the great man. The scene
presented a perfect synthesis between the old and
modern use of public space. Without comment, they
returned to the car and headed back for lunch.

Lunch itself served in the dining room was well
cooked and appreciated but the formality of it
summed up the weekend nicely. Steve went on a roll
and expressed his uptake on what he had seen that
weekend, firstly pointing out that the plaque at the
New Inn hotel indicated that the establishment was
built to accommodate pilgrims visiting the shine
created by monks for the dead Edward the Second.
The income raised and other offerings from pilgrims
at all the churches they visited had helped to build
them. The clerics of these medieval churches seemed
hell bent on acquiring portents and relics to guarantee
financial security. At the root of the history of all the
high culture encountered this weekend were mass
murder, disloyalty and lasciviousness. Families whose
ancestors backed the winning side in those murderess
times probably resided at the top of today's hierarchy.
Whether out of politeness or not, no one disagreed
with this observation.

Thereafter, small talk and giving thanks for the

shown hospitality used up their remaining time together, which ended the one and only time Steve saw the parents of Julia. He knew they were not any different from others used to comfort, and had the means to escape from reality. In this case, to live in a bubble pretending that nothing had changed in the country for the last one hundred years. Julia's parents only saw a rosy past that gave solace to their lives. Everyone had a need to create illusions but haut Anglo-Saxon rural living was not for Steve. Its dull daily routine made it just as much a prison as other walks of life. Their artificially created civilised life rested on a thin crust upon a gigantic charnel pit, which at any moment could bust through the surface. Within this pit, millions upon millions of bodies dumped over millennia in various states of decomposition amalgamated and churned as the active earth stirred them. These remains provided clear forensic evidence of vile painful deaths inflicted on young and old due to overwork, undernourishment, disease and violence. The sweat, toil and blood of this dead seeped into every historic building. For Julia, it was never her home in the first place. It contained nothing of her early childhood or strong evidence of parental love. Nothing in the house suggested any emotional ties: no family portraits, cherished toys, or other memorabilia.

FATE OF THE HARBOUR

The day of the council meeting to finally grant or deny the petition to purchase land to build the marina arrived. The recommendations in the published report on the findings of the delegation that visited the Arabian Gulf had been hugely positive. The town had also beaten off a late challenge from a nearby rival to be the preferred site for it. The late contender was dismissed due to geological reasons. Nevertheless, the keenness in which this town tried to steal the development from Hayes-by-the-Sea highlighted the attraction of such a development to the local populace. For some weeks, PR and marketing teams from up town had embedded themselves in the town to heavily promote the advantages of the development. Their slick charm offensive won over many remaining doubters. The local paper came out in full support of the development as the prospect of reporting on the lives of celebrities rather than the disappearance of a pet was too alluring. The only significant powerful economic voice that continued to raise concerns was from the influential farming lobby. They were worried about the impact of the displacement of their migrant workers from around the harbour area. This would increase costs to them if they had to provide them with better local accommodation or bear the extra transport costs of commuting them from other towns that had suitably available similar low cost poorly maintained housing.

As for Steve, he had received more advice on how to emphasise the additional ecological advantages of the project when the consortium had produced modified plans incorporating recommendations that would enhance the likelihood of acceptance. It was now a two-phase project with the harbour development completed under the first phase with the regeneration of the commercial hub carried out later. In addition, a marina conservation trust would oversee all projects related to the environment and sustainability. The consortium also promised to sponsor the construction of a major contemporary public artwork at a main thoroughfare into town. This will send out a strong message of the seriousness of the town to entice new technologies to relocate here and help boost tourism. Strengthening the town's identity would have extra benefits such as improving the health and wellbeing of the town folk.

Cometh the hour, cometh the woman. Julia continued to speak up and argue against the development despite the onslaught of overt and covert support for it. She was the lone voice in the council chamber that day. She spoke up for all the preservation trusts. Her learnt debating skills were put to excellent use. It was a noble speech about respect for local culture and long-term interests. The seated councillors, the press and the public crammed into the limited space of the viewing gallery could not have been unaffected by her pleas to look beyond today. She stated that the harbour development was a rich man's folly; a fabulous, fanciful and frivolous structure that was alien to its surroundings. She accepted that every generation builds to leave behind their footprint for future generations to see. Nevertheless, good design matures with age allowing it to blend in with the landscape and the history around it. It was designed to decay impressively or in other words become monumental to fit in with the environment. Well-designed structures became eye catchers, an attractive endpoint to a pleasurable journey. This could not be said for these proposals. The scale of this project was monstrous and it would blight the old Georgian town centre. The complex would create severe demands on basic utilities like water. History would record all its silliness, built only for short-term fashionable commercial reasons.

Julia highlighted the flaw in the latest proposal to split the development into separate phases. There was no cast-iron guarantee that all the proposed research work and environmental protection activities would ever happen in phase two. It left the town vulnerable to vested parties with no attachment to the community or interest in enhancing the aesthetic, economic, or cultural qualities of the town. The backers of this development were still unknown, the town had to take the word of city analysts that their intentions were honourable and they genuinely had a long-term interest in the town. The council were the custodians for future generations as well as being responsible for decisions during their period in office. After a couple of years, the novelty of the complex could wear off with the bandwagon moving on to the next *en vogue* attraction. Without its rich backers, the marina management trust would go bankrupt. The town was too small to take over the running of the marina. It was a nightmare just waiting to happen. This was a speculative adventure by capitalists not a generous philanthropic gift from a worldwide benevolent fellowship society. Preserving the history of the town would also be beneficial to house owners, as a massive eyesore next to their properties would devalue prices. If residents turned their backs on heritage the community would lose its cohesion.

The counter-argument spoke about boldness, safeguarding the economic future and the fact that most people lived in post-war red brick housing, not period buildings. Denying the majority a good future was just elitism in its worse form. The town folk required jobs not lectures on aesthetics. The harbour development alone would create four hundred jobs while a revitalised commercial hub would bring in highly paid professional jobs. The region already had fine examples of Georgian period town centres. The only material lost would be the Custom House and some housing along the beach. The harbour was falling down anyway. The development would strengthen the walls on the seafront so protecting the town from possible flooding due to climate change. It was also pointed out that the national government put its full weight behind the proposal, saying it was good for the country that foreign entrepreneurs wanted to establish firm roots in the country. The whole country would benefit from the knock-on effects of such an investment. The construction jobs and the newly acquired skills in using innovative materials would boost the building industry. The closeness of the officer-training academy to the town would ensure that the marina flourished, as the families of the foreign cadets would want to be able to keep in close contact with their kin. If the consortium failed to deliver its promises then the marina could be re-used, say as a naval base. This last comment resulted in unrestrained giggles from the public gallery.

In the end, the environmentalists' vote was not required as the other parties unanimously joined forces to carry the proposal through. In fact, was there was no groundswell of public opinion against this decision. Most residents living in the suburbs only occasionally visited the pebble beach or the old town. They mainly shopped at out of town shopping centres and spent their leisure time at home. Only in the old town was there any real resistance. The residents here were divided between those hoping for higher house prices and others demanding no change to their settled lives. The action of a coalition of other parties to pass the proposal saved Steve from any conflict of interests by allowing him to vote with Julia without any repercussions. His acquiescence up to the time of the vote satisfied the financiers, as they understood the political necessity of his voting decision. Besides, they may need the help of an environmentalist in the future so decided it was best not to rock his boat. The press reported the outcome with zeal, dismissing Julia's pleas as the ravings of the loony left. The only consolation for Julia was that

the official records showed that she exculpated herself
from any future fallout.

Efforts to accelerate the building of the marina
complex resulted in the fast-tracking of import
licences for the acquisition of materials and the
release of employment visas for key workers from
around the world. The finest engineering project
managers were hired to coordinate the multiplicity of
tasks and multitude of workers required to rapidly
complete the huge project. The compulsory purchase
land requests were sent out and quickly accepted as
the consortium paid top dollar for any repossessed
land. The government provided grants to enable
universities and renewable research establishments
to monitor the effectiveness of all the sustainable and
zero carbon energy initiatives. They also made funds
available to build a spur off the motorway to connect
it to the new road east of town. A shantytown of
portacabins appeared overnight on the Downs as
construction work began almost immediately on the
private road and the massive breakwaters. The din of
earthmovers, heavy machinery, drills and men
shouting instructions filled the air from early morning
to dusk. The air was polluted by dust and the sight of
gigantic mechanical swooping cranes shifting a never-
ending supply of pre-fabricated loads from articulated
lorries to their designated resting place. Rubble and
other waste were transported out of the development
to landfill sites hurriedly established just out of town.
The infrastructure of town centre suffered badly as
heavy vehicles had to initially drive through it until
the completed new road relieved this unwanted and
disruptive traffic. The traditional single pane sash

windows of preserved buildings provided poor soundproofing from the rumble of industrial cement mixers, drilling and blasting equipment, bulldozers and fifty-ton articulated lorries that routinely shook up the roads and created potholes.

The presence of over a thousand men living in temporary accommodation in town and on the outskirts of it created the most basic of problems. Outside working hours, the interests of the men orientated towards heavy drinking and the search for quick easy sex. Their personal conduct deteriorated purely because they were miles from home or foreigners with no long-term interest in the town, all miles away from the normal social constraints that held them accountable for their actions. They swamped the local pubs and made unsubtle demands to any female within their vicinity. Many of the young pretty things that once frequented the upmarket bars ran scared of open demands for rough sex. However, some of the great granddaughters of women who in their prime welcomed the arrival of American GIs took up the gauntlet. It was like Christmas had come early for these friendly girls. For some of the unmarried ones, they would have permanent unwanted remainders of this time. For the married ones, it would be a case of mama's baby, papa's maybe.

As there were not enough good-natured volunteers willing to give relief to these hardworking men, entrepreneurs came to the rescue to cater for their needs by shipping in strippers and whores from up town to occupy flats around the bars. Impropriety was clearly visible as half-naked girls paraded their wares. Fast food takeaway shops serving all types of throwaway convenience snacks opened up among the artisan shops. The town then became a magnet for others seeking a good time as it soon acquired a reputation for offering seedy entertainment. Overnight night several pubs re-invented themselves as sports bars. Fights and other disorders were commonplace as supply continually failed to meet demand, or someone did not like the face or the supported football team of another. The police vans' sirens added volume to the incessant jukebox noise and human yells that flooded the night. The mess on the pavements became unbearable. Normally quiet lanes running off the main roads were cluttered with discarded condoms and other sordid items. The perennial debates about dog mess were replaced by the anger of having to continually sidestep the spewed stomach remains of half-digested kebabs, pizzas and fish and chips, all combined with too much consumed ale, the place reeked of urine and vomit. The well-backed propagated message that inconvenience today would bring ample rewards tomorrow failed to reassure the locals. Only the absence of the right to openly defecate on the pavements prevented the old town reverting completely back to Georgian times.

Disenchantment soon became epidemic. The town's good folk deserted the centre at night demanding action to clean it up. The artisans lost trade and they wanted compensation. Decisive action from the authorities remained evasive until the rape of a daughter of a well-connected leading family brought the concerns of the good folk to the attention of the national news media, forcing the authorities to eventually act. The solution was the creation of a fun camp next to the temporary workers' accommodation on the Downs where beer tents, casinos and whores from Eastern Europe provided wild red-light entertainment, all out of sight of the town's good folk.

HELP FOR MI-CHA

As time passed, Steve would eventually inform Julia and Mi-Cha that they would be friends; telling them that it would be better for all of them if they worked as a team. Everyone must know their place and play their part. Their destiny was to become one big happy enterprise, a unit that cared for each other with Steve, of course, at the head.

Prior to meeting each other, Mi-Cha had been told beforehand that her workload would soon be less hectic. The burden of the work placed upon her would be eased. However, it would mean adapting to a new relationship. She could not expect to do less work while expecting everything else to remain the same. He also wanted her to broaden her horizons to gain new experiences. Living in a communal arrangement would intensity life as well as bringing greater financial reward. Polygamy was the order of life before western prudishness condemned it. It was the only setup where women could experience true freedom. It was only denied because the elites believed the masses would not be able to cope with such freedom. Now, we live in an age when all the old hypocrisies have been exposed for what they were, we can do what we craved. In America, the Church of Latter Day Saints was one of the most respected religious orders. Controversy was just a sign of liberation and the demand to express individual rights. It was also an eco-friendlier cohabitation unlike the insular family unit, which only cared about its own interests, wasted resources and discriminated against other lifestyles.

The entrepreneur had been suitably grooming Julia to tolerate being even more liberal in her sexual mores. He explained how all of them living together would finally liberate her from past demons concerning her unloved childhood and severe conservative parents. It would lead to a milieu where she would achieve true sisterhood by the removal of chains imposed by traditional morals. He cited that most revolutions, before being stolen from the people and taken back by the elite masquerading as defenders of the revolution, were happy communal times with shared meals, community bathing and gregarious sexual behaviour. It took some coaxing and force to weaken her resolve to have exclusivity to him but he subdued her. Any past confidante was forgotten, never phoned and emails unanswered. She would continue to be a life coach and a hard-working councillor during the day, but the evenings and nights belonged to Steve.

When finally introduced to each other, it was over dinner in the flat's rustic well-loved kitchen. Julia and Steve first met at a nearby pub and had a casual warm chat together to alleviate any apprehension.

Steve said that Mi-Cha was looking forward to seeing
her and everything was in place for an enjoyable
evening. He quickly explained to her the custom of
cupping her hands when offered soju as a welcoming
drink. Julia, as suggested by Steve, wore a formal
tight black evening dress with black undergarments
and suspendered stockings, all protected against the
elements by a fashionable long black cape. Her hair
was tied back. The height of her black dress shoe
heels was discreet so that she would not appear
threatening to Mi-Cha. Steve just wore his
accustomed smart and colourful cottons with a dark
blue custom-made sporting jacket. After their drink,
they made their way to the flat. Mi-Cha welcomed
them at the door and promptly dealt with their coats
before leading them into the kitchen, her safe domain
where she was in charge.

Julia, a bit nervous and uncertain, immediately sat
down, tended to keep her head down, and only
occasionally attempted to smile at her hosts or offer
polite small talk. On her part, Mi-Cha pre-occupied
herself with the preparation and dishing out of food
while making quick examinations of her new friend
and business colleague. Her attire was less formal and
more suited to the heat of the kitchen, a warm heat
that her Orientale constitution preferred. She looked
delightful in her short-sleeved pink V-neck tee shirt
and blue two-third length chinos that displayed her
thin calves. Her sockless feet were contained within
attractive petite navy-blue gym shoes. A wholesale
bought professional black chef apron protected her
clothing from oil and juice stains from the swiftly
stirred and flipped sizzling hot food.

Mi-Cha facial expressions became thoughtful when she examined their guest, thinking their physiques were similar, both about five feet and lightly framed, so that would help as none of the equipment would need continual re-adjustment, so making everything easy to share. Steve just sat there drinking his wine, smiling broadly, making polite conversation while eyeing the reaction of the women when their eyes made contact with each other or their hands accidentally touched. His main contribution to the evening events was choosing the background music. During the meal, a long-playing recording of various classical compositions reflecting night moods competed with the clatter of utensils. Julia felt hot and clammy, and throughout the meal never completely relaxed. At certain moments, she thought her head was going to explode as mix messages flooded her mind. Swift eye movement betrayed this anxiety. The periodically held hand of Steve from under the table helped to reassure her, stopping her from hurrying her food or rushing out of the flat.

Mi-Cha held her nerve better than Julia due to keeping busy as well as being naturally calmer. She had spent several hours preparing a vegetarian meal of Korean dishes that would suit both women. This entailed cutting, chopping the vegetables beforehand so that only frying and reheating were required when the honoured guest arrived. The entrée was a tart and slightly spicy green salad with apples, grapes and nuts. This was followed by a main meal of stirred fried noodles with sweet potatoes, combined with mushrooms, greens, peppers, carrots and scallions. This was accompanied with side dishes of fried zucchini, fried seaweed, and streamed eggplant and spinach, all well-seasoned. Ginseng tea, mineral water and a selection of wine were permanently available. The dessert was an easy to serve dish of green tea and lime ice cream to aid digestion. If her words did not express it, the effort put into the meal signalled a strong welcome and obedience to Steve's wishes for a good beginning for the new arrangement.

The outcome of their first meeting was never really in doubt as everyone made the effort to enjoy the piping hot food. Mi-Cha explained the main seasoning in each of the dishes, Steve kept the wine glasses full and Julia ate more than she was accustomed. It was a meal that Julia could never have attempted to prepare. Not because it was Oriental but purely because she had no culinary skills. Mi-Cha had grown up in a large family and instinctively gathered skills by observing her grandmother and mother's daily activities in the home. Julia, on the other hand, never had to become adept in the domestic skills. She never learnt to cook or tend a house as she went straight from a boarding school dormitory environment to live within a college hall of residence. After her educational years, she lived alone, ate what she liked without any requirement to adjust to the tastes of others and hired part-time home help to do mundane tasks. The successful meal removed most of the tension and apprehension that existed prior to it. Nonetheless, the awkwardness of the occasion and knowing the expectation of them still dwelled on both women's minds. This led to some self-conscious silences when they tidied up as Steve put on some Leon Cohen music, which hidden speakers relayed throughout the flat.

With formalities over, Steve suggested that Julia
toured the studio to see how the operation worked in
practice. Julia had some idea of what to expect but the
layout surprised her when Mi-Cha opened the
backroom door and invited her in. There had been
months of coaxing from Steve to get her to act out
fantasised desires, admit the sexual preferences she
liked to watch on the Internet and to expand her
sexual experience by training her body to accept
greater exploration and probing. He desired her to
embrace her body, release it and find the freedom it
required without fear of artificial moral constraints.
Nevertheless, as the spotlights were one by one
switched on, she was taken back by the
professionalism of the enterprise. One-half of the
large room had bright lighting flooding a double sized
bed with a camera and a small screen attached above
it on a fixed pole, protruding from the ceiling,
positioned near the foot of the bed. The bed was
slightly tilted upwards so that the camera would not
pick up distorted shaped feet. The interchangeable
panelling behind the bed quickly allowed the
background colour to match the colour of the bed
sheets. The other half of the room was a workshop
with a pottery wheel, moulding equipment and a
small furnace, along with a solid worktop against a
wall that had rows of shelving used to dry out wares.
This sideline to the business manufactured casts of
Mi-Cha's private parts into ceramic *objets d'art*, erotic
drawer handles and the like. They even had their own
range of tried and tested dildos and bum plugs. The
pulling across of a large sound reducing flexible

screen isolated the two activities. On the inside of the backroom door a framed A4 sheet of high-quality paper had the business mission statement boldly displayed: *indiscriminate pleasure for all, not just for the beautiful.*

Steve took Julia over to a laptop to show her some recorded examples of Mi-Cha's performances. The images on the screen were in high definition. This was a high-quality product with no heavy filtering of light or shadows to spoil or cheapen the viewing. The sound equipment was deliberately set to deepen the voice of the performer to make her sound sexier as well as to help camouflage the performer's identity. The conversation with her client was clearly heard. The camera zoomed in and out as if by willpower to perfectly exhibit requested actions. Steve rubbed Julia's lower back and buttocks while explaining how Mi-Cha transmitted the images across the world. Live recordings had conversations and repeated recordings were overlaid with background music, generic music that matched Mi-Cha rhythmic style of movement. They had designed various websites to attract customers from all over the world. The shift work that Mi-Cha had to endure was to enable her to be live at peak trading times in the European, Asian and American markets. They rented time with several major porn sites and had to obey government rules on acceptable acts. If caught breaking guidelines then this lucrative market could be forfeited.

Julia then shared a joint offered by Steve to relax her further. He suggested some still shots to see how her images would appear on the screen. She unzipped out of her black dress to reveal a see-through bra, thong and stockings held up with a suspender belt embossed with little red rose reliefs. Mi-Cha slipped out of her top and bottom to divulge a pink combo of lace bra and pants. Julia approached the bed and hesitantly set herself into what she thought was the expected sexy pose. Instructions then followed on how to appear more natural to the camera. This surprised Julia, as she was half expecting to hear instructions to give more passion. Instead, she was told to remember that the camera would exaggerate any artificial behaviour or expressions. Mi-Cha posed next to her to allow comparisons to be made. The discussion in a matter of fact way about the various shots made her think that her perceived ungainliness and awkwardness was silly. The suggestion for more demanding and risqué shots soon followed. This resulted in the removal of her remaining garments with a naked Mi-Cha jumping onto the bed to demonstrate the stances preferred by the clients. The ice was broken for good when Julia had to spread her knees on the bed while raising her backside high to the camera. This resulted in the release of wind due to the amount of vegetables consumed earlier. Mi-Cha slapped her apprentice's right buttock and blasted out:

"You no good movement, no style!"

The two women laughed and hugged each other. It was all that Steve could have hoped. They decided to stop for the day and decamped to the bedroom to get to know each other more intimately. The women had to learn how to explore each other body and to stir and maintain each other's heightened ecstasy. Steve was the command and control centre, quietly guiding their intertwined movements. He inevitably got aroused and participated in their work out. The tripartite union was consummated. They slept together as one united mass. This postmodern family got off to a good start.

The introduction of Julia would refresh this family business. Previous attempts to add more variety had failed with them reluctantly keeping to a tried and trusted formula that guaranteed to bring income. On one occasion, Steve had attempted to introduce a bondage act but was never satisfied with the results. The off-line recording of him with a PVC mask over his head, penetrating Mi-Cha's body with various appendages just looked clumsy and seedy. Julia would add the necessary variety with a touch of class. They instructed her to hold her hair in a bun and to adorn glasses. Her stage name was Miss Polly, whereas Mi-Cha worked under the pseudonym of Miss Tsai. The latter would retain her customary costume consisting of a sleeveless tight black polo neck top and petite black running bottoms with gym socks. The former would adorn frilly knickers, a short dolly dress and cute laced socks. Two performers diversified the merchandise on sale, created greater choice and allowed shift work to be shared. The screening of double acts expanded their target audience. Additional personnel also meant the operation would maintain its service better as increased staffing improved the capability to cope with sickness or any other unexpected event. Mi-Cha would also have more time to make erotic products, while the mouldings of

Julia's sexual parts would increase the variety on
offer. However, to begin with, Julia had to learn the
ropes by helping off camera and practicing her
fledgeling act until it was second nature to her.

As excellent quality control was the hallmark of any
successful business, Steve did not like his women
hooked on drink, drugs or getting out of shape. He
would not permit them to wear pierced rings or spoil
their bodies with tattoos. They had to look upmarket.
Pubic hair trimmed not completely shaved, as the
shaved look was unreal and ultimately too
anatomical. If he could detect inferior goods then so
would the clients. This meant that Julia from now on
had to become teetotal and drug free like Mi-Cha.

 Julia had to get into good physical shape if she was to
become a valuable asset. Steve instructed Mi-Cha to
develop a fitness plan for her. This meant a daily
routine of exercising. Mi-Cha initiated Julia into the
graceful art of slow stretching movements to improve
her grace and posture. This would de-stress her body
and make it malleable and firm. It would tone up her
abs, back, hips and thighs. She was required to
become a danseuse of the webcam, not to appear as a
rough and ready up town slapper in crotchless
knickers. Soon both were exercising together in the
park, Mi-Cha leading the way with Julia only a split
second behind her movements, stretching to their
limits to improve circulation in the muscles. A happy
body led to a responsive mind. They routinely began
with arms circling and gentle squats, followed by
twists and full limb extension exercises, with knee
and toe bending to apply pressure to the thigh

muscles to strengthen them. Posture holding
movements aided improvement in self-control and
improved balance. The philosophy behind this
exercising conquered fear of change allowing the
participator to move from an imperfect state to a
blissful one. Slow movements between different
stances illustrated the graceful element of their free
open-air performance, with their well-balanced bodies
radiating out health. Mi-Cha was always there to
guide her faithful pupil through difficult spinal or leg
stretches. Holding her pupil's head down on the
ground as her posterior pointed straight up to the
heavens. Julia awkward movements slowly
transformed with her figure into a graceful
representation of a Georgian beauty, slightly anaemic,
slim with an attractive protruding raised bosom.
Steve always insisted that they showered together,
cleaned and dried each other meticulously to maintain
a strong bond.

The new stakeholder always secretly craved to rebel
and soon got addicted to performing sex acts believing
it gave her a sense of power as she controlled the level
of tension and excitement that was passed on to her
paying customer. As her performance improved, she
amassed a quorum of loyal regular followers
necessary for her to become a good asset. Her personal
satisfaction depended on the urges the clients wanted
appeased. It was more rewarding to her if the client
had psychological need of her rather than pure
animalistic ones. She raised her performance when
invited to tease or reprimand the client, whereas,
crude sexual requests were just acted out to order
without any *bona fide* zeal. In comparison, Mi-Cha

gave the same level of performance to every client. Julia's own unique shaped vulva allowed the creation of larger and more winged shaped mouldings. This created a new range of butterfly-like ceramics and bigger erotic handles to allow them to be attached to larger pieces of furniture. Ideally, Julia would do the Americas and some of the Asian markets, and Mi-Cha would concentrate on the European and Asian markets. However, pressures would demand that she did her share of all the markets while double acts meant total visibility as well. In the early days, her role in any double act was a submissive one as Mi-Chi expertly followed online instructions to carry out fantasies on selected parts of Julia's body. Later, she would take a leading role as well, becoming expert in the use of lubricants and the manipulation of different sex toys to safely widen the cavity that the client demanded to be explored.

All this online activity meant despite the precautions to hide Julia's identity a significant probability of being recognised was there, especially if watched by someone who was in daily contact with her. This eventually happened but, despite several hours of blind panic, turned out favourable in the end. A fellow councillor would spot her while cruising webcam sex sites one drunken night when he was bored out of his skin. As his wife was downstairs catching up on late night repeats of her favourite soaps he sat in his upstairs makeshift office paying premium rates to get girls to talk dirty and expose themselves. He initially recognised Julia by lamely reflecting that the earlobes of this hostess looked similar to those of someone with whom he had a recent boring one-to-one meeting. He laughed out loud when he finally recognised her then proceeded to undress and sent a nude erected phallic selfie of himself to the advertised twitter account, suggesting they should meet up for some fun. A panicking Julia swapped places with the resting Mi-Cha then rushed to inform Steve of the terrible news.

Steve took it all in his stride by texting back to the councillor that if he did not register a payment of one thousand pounds to their website payment account then the national press would receive his obscene photo. The threat of disgrace resulted in the demanded payment. When viewer and performer later met in the flesh, the blackmailed councillor never publicly maligned Julia and once she got used to his reluctant silence she actually enjoyed the power of tease over him. The forever looking for a profit Steve then passed on the photo of the councillor to his spymasters. The resultant financial reward pleasantly surprised him. From there on in, he encouraged his girls to get clients to send compromising photos, which they would compare with official portraits of local councillors, MPs, MEPs and Members of the Lords. Full approval from his spymasters of this new sideline was confirmed when they sent him surveillance and spyware tools. Photo recognition software to speed up identification checks along with a database of faces they were keen to have good incriminating gossip on, allowing them to compromise these individuals to use them for their own ends. Spyware allowed full access to upload all information held on these client's devices. The security services also advised Steve not to attempt to extort too much but instead demand that they pay long-term membership to his webcam site. This way the victims could be hooked while at the same time not living in fear of being financially crippled, which could force some of them to suddenly find moral principles. If pushed too far into a corner, some may publicly confess their misdemeanours.

Steve would never intentionally be financially mean to his ladies. So long as it never interfered with his own adventures, they could spend as much money as desired. Greed was never one of his sins. He only unfailingly carried out two out of the seven deadly sins, lust and gluttony, which was probably not bad given all the temptations available. He just lived a life completely independent of obligations and never retreating from reality or failing to live the moment. As for his companions, by luck or design, they were always too busy to take significant leave to enjoy the extravagances that Steve relished when he disappeared for days on end to visit or try out new exotic pleasures. They would just continue to work assiduously away together during his leaves of absence. Whether he was present or not the money rolled in. The two women were self-reliant. Nonetheless, both felt the need to maintain the support of a male lead.

Inadvertently their leader brought together human beings that developed a fondness for each other, giving these industrious angels a shared purpose in life. Mi-Cha by temperament was reserved rather than expressive, unaggressive yet resistant to break loyalties and stood no nonsense from strangers whereas, in her girlish reveries, Julia craved sweet uncomplicated companionship. The women themselves instinctively became umbilically attached and devoted to keeping the unit together. They became lovers, friends, confidantes and a source of help when required. Everything a relationship required. They were like binary stars rotating about a common axis as they lived in perfect harmony with one and other, never encroaching in each other's chosen fortes. A picture of Mi-Cha with Julia had a place of honour on the large American fridge with the rest of the family photographs. In truth, they no longer required the presence of Steve. Observed by the outside world, they were emancipated women taking advantage of the relaxation in society of the private sexual mores of women. The sex trade was a flourishing cottage industry and they did not feel degraded by offering their services. As wage earners, they earned more than Steve did, and far more than most working people as well. They did not even have to earn a living, as money received through family ties would suffice them.

Mi-Cha took great pleasure in making sure the world saw an immaculately turned out Julia, as each morning she pruned and shaped her eyelashes, cleansed and applied makeup to her face. At spare moments at night, she would enjoy manicuring her hands, feet and nails. Julia dress sense became more flamboyant as she wore the same flimsy undergarments on all occasions while her body radiated fitness and confidence. High heeled shining shoes, tighter fitting fine wool business dresses, loose silk tops revealing the top of her bra finished off with an expensive silk scarf draped across the shoulders became the norm. Her richly dyed golden blond hair was slightly starched to emphasis her political credentials. She swapped her eco-friendly Toyota Prius for a matching Alfa Romeo, always keeping expensive hand creams and perfume in the glove compartment. She would acquiesce her support for Steve by accrediting him for saving the seafront; safeguarding the environment from any industrialisation to ensure its future would continue to be a seafaring one. He became a modern day political enigma: a locally acclaimed progressive thinker whose silence could be bought. As for Mi-Cha, she continued to be the rock on which the whole enterprise was built. Her quiet hardworking nature meant she was always busy in the background. She kept the business up to date by successfully keeping pace with emerging technology and social media trends.

The harbour development and the promise public artwork on a main roundabout into town were completed. The glass towers of postmodernity had, as expected, a mixed reception. One caused significant light population as the island hotel with its piazza and restaurants lit up the bay at night, while the other dazzled commuters at rush hour. The stars were blanked out by the lights from the hotel, the condominiums and the promenade along with the sweeping beams of light from warning beacons at the perimeter of the breakwaters to mark the entrance to the marina. The reflections off the sea and the nearby chalk cliffs created a broad eerie fluctuating glow around this bright centre. In town at sunset and sunrise the glare from the myriad of steel and glass shards that replaced the oasis for flora and fauna at the centre of the old roundabout blinded traffic to such an extent that the structure had to finally be painted over which turned it into an opaque nothingness. The second phase of the project to encourage eco-friendly companies to relocate into the commercial hub never materialised, it was quietly dropped after the completion of an obtuse electrified security fence and a water-filled ditch around the marina complex. The latter managed to get through the planning stage because it was presented as a flood protection overflow channel. The expected hundreds of new jobs for locals was another casualty of early promises, as an accommodation ship unexpectedly moored on the outer side of one of the breakwaters to house cheap foreign labour from the Philippines and Asia.

A plan to move out of the flat to cohabitate in Julia's Georgian house never happened. The upheaval seemed too demanding so they happily resided in the flat, it was comfortable and engendered an intimacy that the other dwelling may have diffused. Nevertheless, the house would remain a significant jewel in the crown and would eventually bring in substantial revenue. It would be used as a location for video shots, a continued base for Julia's occasional lifestyle coaching and a formal residence to meet fellow councillors or party central office officials when they ordained to visit the provinces. More importantly, in the summer months it would be rented out to a new type of tourist who was attracted by the smell of wealth that engulfed the marina. The amazing rental value of the house reflected the

astronomical rise in house prices throughout the
historic old town. The earlier purchase of buy-to-let
flats using finance from Mi-Cha's father repaid big
dividends almost immediately. For Steve, the elevated
position within the family naturally increased his
sense of his self-importance and superiority. Once fed
rich food, the ego seeks out more. He began to believe
everything he said, becoming accustomed to expecting
the best service available. There would be no need to
report to the job centre for clandestine meetings, as a
personal minder was assigned to him with invites to
lunch up town for face-to-face informal meetings.
When going up town to a pre-arranged meeting, he
would travel up the night before for an appointment
with a high-class whore in Mayfair. Her worktop was
a four-poster period bed draped in silk with a ceiling
mirror. His sessions were probably being recorded but
hell he did not care. He particularly enjoyed sitting
nude by a real fire nestled in a luxurious armchair
with a glass of excellent port in his hand, a Cuban
cigar smoking away in an ashtray on a side table,
stroking the hair of the amiable girl then smelling her
scent on his hand as she fellated him. No man was
happier than him on such occasions. The next
morning, he would see his tailor to update his
wardrobe then spend several hours at a sauna being
pampered by girls rubbing fine oils into his skin and
manicuring his hands. This gave him a well-cut high-
class appearance, which would become more formal
and less artisan looking.

On a rare occasion, he would arrange to meet Jason
up town on the pretext to mend broken bridges and
find out how things were going. One was tired of

what up town had become and the other still saw it as a circus to enjoy. The increased bustle on the streets due to the multitude of foreign voices and faces when they relocated themselves between pubs was just too overbearing for Jason. He now only found sanctuary in drinking hostels, which seemed to him to be the last bastions held by the nation, settings where he did not feel like an alien. The conversations of both men betrayed their normal lack of tack. Steve just instinctively loved to needle his old friend. Knowing Jason's penchant for pretentiousness, he spared no effort to impress him to put him in his place. He deliberately embarrassed him by taking him to an upmarket cocktail lounge that would cripple his finances when it came to his round, all the time taking delight in observing his discomfort as his dishevelled attire stood out against the well-tailored clientele in the bar. The black fine cotton suit that Jason always wore shone in the light due to its age and state of wear while his dark shirt showed signs of fraying at the collar. The waiters all had superior clothing compared to him. As Steve thoroughly enjoyed being a pompous ass, Jason's world seemed to be collapsing within its self with his subjects of conversation coming across as mundane and xenophobic. He moaned about the rise of Islam with the unwelcomed influence of Middle East and Asian born Imams spreading their message of hatred in this country. Steve stirred it up by reminding him that most Catholic priests here came from the Republic of Ireland. Finally changing the subject, Jason would make it known that no one had heard from Martin in years. The assumption was that he was dead. Steve said he would ask his contacts to ascertain his whereabouts or to confirm the worse. Jason never really understood what this comment meant, attributing it to idle pub talk. In Jason's world ignoramuses like Steve always took on airs and false grandiose confidence for the most trivial of reasons. He still bitterly remembered the day in southern Italy when wandering around a local farmers' market Steve whistled to him to keep up as if he was a dog. The evening ended in predictable disharmony with the resumption of hostilities. The only possible good outcome from this soiree was the slight possibility of finding out what happened to Martin. Both of them realised that they did not have much in common apart from being friends in their youth when friendships were taken for granted.

When invited to the new private marina complex Steve would be one of many joyful regular vacuous guests at the gatherings of the super-rich. He easily mixed with the Arab, Russian and Asian billionaires who frequented the marina without any feeling of inferiority or jealousy, even strolling around with the economy of movement that the rich seemed to possess. He always pronounced himself as a property developer at such gatherings. His lifelong held attitude of seeing money only as a commodity to allow him to have fun and not something that was hard earned enabled him to fit comfortably in this milieu, a privileged milieu suitable for the commanders of today's global interests. The difficult to get into marina was a suitable rendezvous for the world's elite. It was not only a pleasure dome but also a court that the country's heads came to pay their respect. With power came responsibility. The global leaders of the asset class with unlimited supply of money and other resources had to make hard decisions; a powerful oligopoly of high-ranking men capable of weakening any state economy and wiping out hundreds of thousands of jobs by just shifting money out of it. A memorable highlight for Steve would be a good chat with the Asian owner of a global empire that manufactured his favourite car. A car Steve now preferred to be seen driving. Government cabinet members down for the weekend to mix business with pleasure would mistake Steve for one of the super-rich and attempt to get him to give donations to their party. This was not surprising as his rounder figure and tanned well-moisturised skin gave him an Eastern Mediterranean appearance while his tactile friendly mannerism blended in well to enhance his credentials. He always smiled at their flatulent pleading. He particularly took a liking for the energy secretary who attempted to flatter him by pointing out that history indicated that the best gentlemen in this country were invariably foreign born.

Top sports personalities and A-list celebrities flocked to the complex, where they bought or leased the luxury apartments along the redeveloped shore. Again, it was a case of mixing business with pleasure, as it was important for these people to maintain a high profile and to be seen with the owners and sponsors of all the major sport and entertainment events. Their arrival enhanced the profile of the marina. This influx was a big factor in getting the public to accept the value of such a project to the nation, as they perceived the place not to be a foreign rich man's paradise but a resort for their beloved celebrities to relax in.

The marina reception bars were always buzzing with high-class chitchat. Guests drinking expensive cocktails and munching canapés and other hors d'œuvres created up town and flown in especially that day, while dyed blond haired want-to-be supermodels mingled about only too glad to exploit their looks and bodies to gain the trappings of prestige and luxury. Posh totty on the make that knew they had a short shelf life. The best many of these girls would achieve was a walk-on part in some major movie production paid by an influential sponsor, allowing them to wiggle their prize assets for a few seconds, whether it was their bosom or backside. Nonetheless, it could be very lucrative for a few of them if they snared a rich benefactor. All they had to be for a limited time until a younger model came along was beautiful, compliant and obedient; real life intimating art by being Stepford Wives for the super-rich. It was not always cream that rose to the top, and being in the presence of the super-rich who spurted opulence in this crystal palace with panoramic views of the Channel, chalk cliffs and the magnificent state of the art marina, the returning to earth droplets of riches wetted Steve's lips for more.

The strange thing about the material success bestowed on Steve was he never really understood the theories behind wealth accumulation. Despite this, he did not let his lack of understanding confuse him; he just let it go without a second thought. He did come to a simple conclusion about others citizens, that in their own way they were all mad. He had seen various manners of living, observing at first hand the motivations of the participants to toil away to preserve their own particular way of life. He had experienced the direct unabashed speech of the working poor and the polite but fundamentally honest disinterest in others conversations of the more comfortable classes. Simply put, he never fathomed out why so many accepted the role given to them or adopted the expected persona instead of rebelling against it. These people seemed to accept a restrictive existence fearing the absence of toiling to maintain it would result in a worse outcome. They all seemed to suffer from the misfortune of possessing virtue. Whereas the rich never worried or questioned how they obtained wealth, they only sought to possess it so they could manipulate its power, while celebrities enhanced their standing with the media and subsequently their popularity by being notorious to get attention. The highest priority for them was to make sure that the only path followed was the shortest one that brought maximum personal gain. The more gained the higher your standing, reputation and position within society. All the winners enjoyed abundant free time to relish in their pleasures. This contrasted with the taught attitudes of many, leading them to think that the way they earned a living mattered. Maybe, that ex-statesman he met was not wrong after all. The role of modern leaders was to carry the guilt of those who benefitted from injustices, relieving them of their sins that contributed to the creation of an unfair society and to reluctantly accept the blame when unfavourable economic conditions periodically rocked and rattled safe comfortable havens built by a toiling electorate.

As for the redoubtable recipient of prodigious rewards, all the signs seemed to indicate that more riches were coming. The extra profit from Julia's contributions and the increase in the arrangement fee from the security services for his surveillance work meant they would inevitably become a multi-million-pound enterprise. A mention in a future New Year's honours list for services rendered to the nation was even hinted at. He was a man of his time, shallow and doing well out of the labours of others. The man could have anything he desired. He had his own following, money, Georgian period properties, two harlots and a promised place in the established order of society. He even bought a genuine expensive work of art by an uncredited Italian medieval painter, thought to be a pupil of Giotto. It was a small tempera painting on wood several inches squared depicting a close-up upper body foreground image of Christ appearing to be conducting a sermon with Saint Peter and Saint Mathew, either side and slightly behind him. He got it encased within a reflection-free glass case and hung it above the bed of his performers to remind him of past friends and the so-called intellectual arguments they had about art when he had visited Tuscany in his youth. Beside this artefact, he hung a replicated tempera portrait of himself with Mi-Chi and Julia, standing behind and either side of him.

"Life can take you to unexpected places, Anonymous"